Mexico 1968... Student uprising destroyed

1971... remaining movement handled down

1977... economic boom.
left then disappeared

1973... Chilean govern-
ment overthrown
→ repression

1976: Argentinian
military gov

Noir Detective an
Mexican / Latin
American

Narrative that mexican
readers can relate to
→ created a model for
future writers

# An Easy Thing

epigraphs from writers
a leftist would read
→ hopeful
→ Chandler and
other exceptions

hoped to help Mexico
accept its gay populat-
ion, although he does
it in a problematic
way → at a time
when these topics were
not explored

Hector as a poverty
tourist

community

radio show → intervening
politically

Hector's family

he communities, like the one created
in the radio, are imagined. Don't have
much in common
and will not
actually meet the
majority of them

revolution... looking for
change where there
seems to be none.

D0869308

**The Héctor Belascoarán Shayne Detective Novels**
By Paco Ignacio Taibo II
Translated by William I. Neuman
*An Easy Thing*
*Some Clouds*
*No Happy Ending*

Translated by Laura Dail
*Return to the Same City*

# An Easy Thing

A Héctor Belascoarán Shayne Detective Novel

## Paco Ignacio Taibo II
translated by William I. Neuman

Poisoned Pen Press

1977

Copyright © 1990, 2002, 2013

Trade Paperback Editions 2002, 2013

10 9 8 7 6 5 4 3 2

Library of Congress Catalog Card Number: 2001098491

ISBN: 9781590580066     Trade Paperback

Poisoned Pen Press
6962 E. First Ave., Ste. 103
Scottsdale, AZ 85251
www.poisonedpenpress.com
info@poisonedpenpress.com

Printed in the United States of America

To the rest of the Full House: Toño Garst *El Biznaga*, Toño Vera *El Cerebro*, Paco Abaradía *El Quinto*, and Paco Pérez Arce *El Ceja*; in memory of that afternoon we played volleyball instead of studying Lenin's *What Is to Be Done?*

The poet David Eshner started the translation of this novel into English in 1985, but he was unable to finish because of his untimely death. Although the translation by Willie Neuman is completely new, some of the ideas and the spirit of Eshner remain in it.

# Note to the North American Edition

Only one figure survives as a popular hero seventy years after the Mexican Revolution. This is Emiliano Zapata, peasant leader from the southern state of Morelos, who was murdered in an ambush in 1919 on the Chinameca Ranch.

Zapata's image, his picture, his words, resurface again and again in the history of Mexico. He is, perhaps, the most important figure in contemporary Mexican history, as well as the central mythological figure of the failed revolution.

# Chapter One

There is only hope in action.
—J. P. Sartre

"One more, boss," said Héctor Belascoarán Shayne.

For half an hour, he'd stood with his elbows anchored to the bar, letting the time slip by, his eyes wandering nowhere in particular, interrupting the bustle of his thoughts every now and then to order another drink. The *cantina* was called The Lighthouse at the End of the World. It was a high-class dive located inside the old feudal city of Azcapotzalco, in what had once been the outskirts of Mexico City, but was now just another link in an endless chain of industrial zones, where the picturesque remains of haciendas, graveyards, and village churches stood in the shadow of a monstrous oil refinery, the pride of fifties technology.

He drained the last drop from his glass and accepted a fresh one from the bartender. From the beginning, he'd been emptying the rum on the sawdust-covered floor and pouring Coke into the glass, spiking it with a twist of lime. These virgin *cuba libres* saved him the embarrassment of not drinking liquor in a *cantina*. Besides which, the little game amused him.

All around him, a group of village musicians were getting mercilessly wasted on *mezcal* and *tequila*. They'd come to town looking for work, but didn't find any, and were celebrating their bad luck. Between rounds and rounds and rounds and rounds, they played old songs spiced up with a few asthmatic trombones and cheap, tinny-sounding trumpets.

The din grew louder.   rum and coke

He asked for another *cuba libre* and poured the rum on the floor. "This makes seven," he told himself, not knowing for certain whether he was really thirsty or whether he simply just wanted to keep the binging musicians company. The only problem was, in that environment, even his fictitious drinks were starting to have a psychological effect.

"*Don* Belascoarán?" inquired a hoarse voice in the midst of the tumult.

Héctor emptied his glass and left the bar, following the man with the hoarse voice. They wound their way through the crowd of drunk musicians, prostitutes, and refinery workers gearing up for the weekend—toward that same lonely table that stands in the back of every Mexican *cantina*, as if it's waiting for the great Pedro Infante, strumming his guitar and dressed like a Mexican *charro*, to walk in and claim it as his own. The stranger dropped into one of the chairs, waiting for Héctor to do the same before removing his cowboy hat and depositing it on another chair nearby.

"I got a little job for you." The man was about fifty years old. He had dreamy gray eyes set in a face of proud, noble features. A two-inch scar ran across his sunbaked forehead.

Héctor nodded.

"But first…first I have to tell you a story. It's an old story and it starts where the history books end…in 1919 on a *hacienda* in Chinameca, with the murdered body of Emiliano Zapata laid out on the ground and the flies eating at his eyes…or at least the body *of the guy who they thought was Emiliano.*"

The old man paused to drain his glass of *tequila.*

"Because, you see, Emiliano never went to the *hacienda.* He knew what his enemies were like, and he knew how far he could trust them. He ended up sending this buddy of his who wanted to go in his place. The guy kept insisting, and so Emiliano sent him just to keep him off his back. He's the guy that got shot out there at the ranch. Emiliano went into hiding and watched the Revolution die…It wasn't like him to do that, but, you see, he'd lost his self-confidence, he'd lost faith…he didn't want to go on any more. So, like I said, he went underground. Then in 1926 he met this Nicaraguan guy working for the Huasteca

Petroleum Company in Tampico. Emiliano was a quiet guy. You couldn't get him to say a word. What had happened to the revolution, well, you know, it had taken something out of him. He was forty-seven years old at the time, and the Nica was only twenty-eight. The guy's name was Sandino. They went together to Nicaragua to fight against the *gringos*. And they fought 'em good, too. If you look carefully you can see him in some of those old pictures, kind of off to the side in one of the corners, like he doesn't want to be seen, almost like he isn't even there… But when it came down to giving the *gringos* a little bit of hell, you can bet he was in there with the best of 'em. Yessir. He'd learned a lot in the revolution, and he put it to good use. But the deal came down in Nicaragua, too, and Sandino got killed. Now the pictures are the only proof that Emiliano was there… After Nicaragua he came home to Mexico, holed up in a cave, and wouldn't eat. He was ready to die there, alone.

"But the people found him and they wouldn't let him starve. They brought him food and took care of him. The years slipped by. Then Rubén Jaramillo started organizing again, and *don* Emiliano gave him advice. They would spend hours in the cave together, talking…And then the bastards killed Jaramillo. *Don* Emiliano came out to visit his friend's grave and then went back to his cave for good.

"And that's where he is today…He's still there, he's still there."

The surrounding hubbub finally broke the bubble of silence that enclosed Belascoarán and the man with the scar. With three of their members sleeping it off under a table, the rest of the orchestra let loose with a tearful *bolero* dominated by the wind instruments' sorrowful wail. A couple of dozen regulars filled the bar, at that hour mostly workers from a small foundry on the corner, and as the band played on, a hush fell over the crowd and the men's faces grew serious. Even the domino players stopped rattling the bones, and slid the pieces silently across the marble tabletops.

"What's it got to do with me?" asked the detective. He had lived his whole life in a city where the legend of Zapata had never managed to break free from the hollowness of the towering monuments or the frozen metal of the statues. The warm sun that shone in the state of Morelos, Zapata's old stomping grounds, had never broken through the gray horizon of Mexico City's rain-streaked Septembers. But all the same, Héctor wanted to believe. He longed to see the heroic Zapata, now ninety-seven years old, charging up the avenues of the city on his white horse, filling the wind with his bullets.

"What's it got to do with me?" he asked again.

"I want you to find him," rasped Scar-face, producing a leather bag which he set gently onto the table.

Héctor guessed at its contents: gold coins, doubloons, silver from the Spanish Empire. But he didn't touch the bag, and he was careful to keep his eyes off it. Intrigued as he was by the old man's story, he still tried to think of it as just another hallucination. Just another one of his many, so typically Mexican hallucinations.

"What if it's all a lie?"

"Then prove it to me. I want proof," answered Scar-face, getting up from the table. He downed another shot of *tequila* and walked away.

"Hey, wait a minute," Héctor called in the direction of the swinging doors as the orchestra ended the *bolero* and broke for the bar.

Héctor picked up the bag and stowed it safely in the inner pocket of his gabardine coat. Outside, the rain came down in sheets, slapped at his face, and soaked his hair. He couldn't see for more than fifteen feet.

"*Puta madre,*" he swore under his breath, "the guy wants me to find Emiliano Zapata."

The noise of the rain drowned out the noise from The Lighthouse at the End of the World. Héctor stepped farther out into the storm, picking his way between the puddles, trying to avoid the streams of water that cascaded from drainpipes over the street.

His thoughts were full of the sun shining over the state of Morelos, the sun that had once shone on the face of Emiliano Zapata.

The taxi dropped him in front of the Herrera Funeral Home. Yellowish lights lit the street and cast a luminous glow around the place. The storm had dissipated, but puddles still dotted the street, brimming with reflections. A pair of old men shuffled past Héctor as he went inside, and he strained to catch a few words in the whispered conversation that trailed off behind them like a tail. Two hearses stood in the courtyard, along with a florist's pickup unloading funeral wreaths.

"Room number three?" he asked the receptionist.

He followed a pair of arrows set on posts, into a large salon filled with a yellowish light, where a steel-gray coffin rested on a marble tabletop. Its silent presence dominated the room.

Héctor looked around. His aunts, dressed in black, sat in the corner opposite the door, whispering among themselves. His sister, Elisa, stood alone, with her back to the coffin, staring out a darkened window at the last scattered drops of rain. His brother, Carlos, sat near the door, with his head between his hands, while the maid and the gardener from the house in Coyoacán sat two chairs farther on, dressed rigorously in black. The family lawyer stood in front of the coffin, conversing in hushed tones with a representative of the funeral home.

Héctor approached the coffin and lifted the lid. There was a serenity to the face that he hadn't seen for many years. The long gray hair fell around her neck, and a Spanish *mantilla* covered her head. A gift from his father, it served as a reminder of those terrible years.

"Good-bye, Mama," he whispered.

And now what? What do you do now? Do you cry because your mother's dead? Do you try to bring back the memories of closeness and love? Try somehow to search your unconscious for that spinal recollection of earliest childhood? Do you play

the games again? Do you ignore the bad times, the fights, the
scoldings, the unbridgeable distance of recent years?

Do you cry? Is it best to cry, even just a little bit, shaking the
dust from forgotten feelings until the tears come? Or is it better
to say *So long*, and walk away?

Héctor closed the lid and went out.

Outside again, in the patio, he stopped to watch the workers
unloading flowers from the pickup truck, and lit a cigarette. A
pair of tears stained his cheeks.

Elisa came up beside him, sliding her hand around his upper
arm. For a long time they stood together in silence, not looking
at each other, starting straight ahead. Later on they sat down on
a set of steps leading onto the central courtyard. It had stopped
raining.

"The damn lawyer wants the three of us to meet him in
his office tomorrow at six P.M.," announced Carlos, lighting a
cigarette as he joined them. "Was it the same when Papa died?"
he asked after a brief silence.

"You don't remember?"

"How old was I? Six?"

"Yeah, I guess so…It was worse then, a lot worse. Papa was
a lot closer to us, and we were younger then, too. It was different," Héctor explained.

"Death is different now," said Elisa, and Héctor felt her hand
tighten around his arm.

*So long, Mama*, he thought. It's all over now. You don't have
to worry any more about the time passing by, no more lonely
nights in your man's big empty house, no more pictures to look
at from when you sang for the internationalists in Spain, or when
you performed your Irish folk songs in New York City, no more
nostalgia, no more worrying over your beautiful, bright red hair
gone gray. No more wayward children you can't understand.
That's it, the show's over, you did it all. It was worth it.

Was it worth it? he wondered.

"Fucking death. Fuck everybody who has to die this way,"
he said.

◇◇◇

He dropped down onto the unmade bed. Unmade since yesterday and the day before, unmade until tomorrow, and the day after, and the day after that, until his disgust finally compelled him to make it again, to smooth sheet against sheet, to fight back against the invincible wrinkles, to beat the lumps out of the pillow (deposited there by who knows what mysterious process), and to shake the ancient dust from the beautiful Oaxacan blanket which was the only luxury he allowed himself, the only aesthetic concession he was willing to make in that tiny room with bare walls and bald furniture.

He rubbed his fingertips against his aching temples. After hesitating for a moment, he got up from the bed and walked wearily, like a man with a pair of incompatible ideas crowding the space inside his head, to the corner of the room where he'd dropped his gabardine trench coat. No matter what I do to it, it always ends up looking like a rag, he thought fondly. From one of its inner pockets, he pulled the wrinkled envelope he'd been carrying around all day. He studied it carefully. His office address was written in a steady, round hand, beneath a set of Italian stamps displaying a sepia-tinted image of the Coliseum. A larger, modish-looking special-delivery stamp added a sense of urgency.

Héctor weighed the envelope in his hand, opened it slowly, and dropped back onto the bed.

> I started out hoping that I'd be able to tell you what I'm doing here, and before I'd even written the first line I knew that I'd never never never never never never be able to explain any of it. As if there was anything to explain! Now I know there's no such thing as escape, and that a journey has no end at all, but only a beginning. What are you running from? What am I running from? When you're running away from yourself, then there's nowhere to go, no place is safe, there's nowhere to hide. You look in the mirror

and see the person you're running away from right there in front of you every day.

What do I do? you ask, How do I spend my time? I couldn't even tell you. Sometimes something touches me, breaks through, leaves a mark: a certain person, a glass of chianti, a plate of veal with red peppers, a glimpse of the sea…But mostly the hours fly by, all so much alike, all so different, all so damn meaningless. Now you see them, now you don't. I'll bet the enemy knows what to do with them.

I sleep a lot.

I sleep alone.

Mostly.

Shit, I wasn't going to say anything.

I walk all the time. Like a madwoman. Who knows, maybe I am.

I love you. IloveyouIloveyouIloveyouIloveyou

Still chasing after stranglers?

Send me a map of Mexico City, and mark all the streets where we used to walk, and the parks, and the bus routes. Mail me a Metro ticket, and a picture of my race car. Send me a picture of you on San Juan de Letrán, walking along at exactly five o'clock in the afternoon, like on that day.

Pretty soon I'll get bored with running away from myself and then we can see each other again.

Will you wait for me?

—ME

He read it again, from beginning to end, line by line. Then he took a look at the photograph, the Italian bus token, the map of Venice, the newspaper clipping, the napkin with the lipstick kiss.

He went back to the photo: a lonely woman in a lonely street. A fruit seller in the distance gave it a more human perspective. She wore a long black dress with a high collar and wide, flowing skirt, black boots with inlaid bits of color. In one hand she held a folded newspaper, a long-stemmed carnation in the other. Her brightly smiling face, in three-quarter profile, her hair gathered into the familiar ponytail at the back of her head.

He hesitated and then stuck the photograph on the windowsill, wedging a corner into a small crack between the sill and the pane of glass.

The face in the picture smiled sweetly at him, and finally, Héctor Belascoarán Shayne, detective by trade, replaced the furrowed brow and poker face he'd worn all day long with a weak smile.

Life goes on.

Walking into the kitchen, he turned on the radio, heated some oil in a pan, and started to chop up tomatoes and onions for a steak *à la mexicana*. He found some chiles in the refrigerator, and as he salted and peppered the steak, he thought about his life.

It was a joke. Just one hell of a big joke. Thinking that he could be a detective in Mexico. It was crazy. There was nothing else like it, nothing to compare it to. But when, in the course of six short months, there had been six different attempts on his life (with a scar to show for every one of them), when he had won 64,000 pesos on a television quiz show, when there were days when a small line of potential clients formed in his office (well, okay, so two people make a line); and better yet, when he had managed to solve (drumroll, please) the famous case of construction fraud at the Basilica, as well as the mysterious death of the goalie from the Jalisco soccer team; and more than that, having managed just to survive all those months and still take it all so seriously, and to take it lightly, too, but seriously above all—then, and only then, did the joke cease to be a joke on him alone, and it became part and parcel of the city itself, of the whole damn country even.

If there's one thing this country won't forgive you for, it's that you take your life too seriously, that you can't see the joke.

*Damn loneliness.*

Damn loneliness, he thought, turning off the stove.

And during the same six months, in Veracruz, the army had run a group of starving squatters off a fruit plantation belonging to an ex-president of the republic.

Mama shouldn't have gone and died.

I shouldn't still be playing at cowboys and Indians.

And yet, what else was there to do? What better way to live this crazy life than to jump right into the frying pan, just like that juicy steak *à la mexicana*.

Is Zapata still alive?

The radio caught his attention for a moment:

> *Nosotros,*
> *Que desde*
> *que nos vimos*
> *amándonos estamos…*
> *Nosotros*
> *que del*
> *amor hicimos*
> *un sol maravilloso*
> *romances…*
>
> You and I,
> From the very
> first time we met,
> we knew it had to be love…
> You and I,
> we took our love
> and made from it
> a brilliant shining sun…

It was far better, after all, than to be forever chasing the dollar, a new car, the needle-dick life, middle-class security, tickets to the symphony, neckties, cardboard relationships, cardboard sex in a cardboard bed, the wife, the kids, upward mobility, a salary, a career; the rat race he had fled from suddenly one day six months ago to go hunt down a strangler. A killer who in the end he found mirrored inside himself.

Is Emiliano Zapata still alive?

He burned his hand taking the frying pan off the stove.

Mama, why'd you have to go and die?

The woman with the ponytail smiled at him from the windowsill.

Shit, is this what they call *taking stock of your life?*

*Nosotros,*
*debemos separarnos*
*no me preguntes*
*maaás.*
*No es falta*
*de cariño…*

You and I,
It's time for us to part,
don't ask me questions
any more.
It's not for lack
of affection…

sang the radio.

Héctor Belascoarán Shayne made a face and stuck out his tongue, as he set a sizzling steak *à la mexicana* on the kitchen table.

Stuttering badly, the elevator carried Héctor up from the dazzling sunshine of the street to the bluish half-light of the third-floor landing. He walked over to his office door, and paused in front of the metal shingle that read:

*HÉCTOR BELASCORÁN SHAYNE: DETECTIVE*
*GILBERTO GÓMEZ LETRAS: PLUMBER*
*"GALLO" VILLAREAL: SEWER AND DRAINAGE SPE-*
*CIALIST*
*CARLOS VARGAS: UPHOLSTERER*

The sign greeted him every morning, a constant reminder not to take things too seriously. After all, what self-respecting *film noir* detective would share an office with a sewer expert, an upholsterer, and a plumber?

"Looks like a fucking tenement house," he thought.

Smiling weakly, he opened the squeaky door and stepped inside. He hung his leather jacket with the copper buttons on the coatrack, and thought again about his decision not to dress in black. The smile disappeared from his face.

Things had changed drastically since his last visit. A stack of skeletal, partially upholstered furniture was piled up in one corner, blocking the window, and two new desks had appeared, filling the empty space and completely rearranging the geometry of the room. Yet, in spite of the overall changes, his own things had been left undisturbed: a secondhand desk; two old chairs bought on the cheap from a movie lot, looking exactly as if they belonged in a detective's office; a dilapidated file cabinet, its varnish peeling; the tear-off calendar, showing the date from a week ago; the coatrack; the ancient black telephone.

He dropped into his chair, and pulled the cord on the venetian blind. It fell noisily into place, breaking the morning into hard strips of light.

A note waited for him on his desk:

PLEASE CONSIDER POSSIBLE ADDITION OF PINUP OF MECHE CARREÑO IN MONOKINI. APPROVED BY ACCLAMATION IN VOTE BY OFFICE MATES.
PS: SORRY TO HEAR ABOUT YOUR MOTHER.

PPS: YOU IDIOT! IF YOU'RE GOING TO LEAVE YOUR
DAMN GUN AROUND THE OFFICE, REMEMBER TO
PUT THE SAFETY ON!

—GILBERTO, GALLO, CARLOS

He smiled wistfully, letting his eyes drift around the room until
he spotted the bullet hole made by his .38 in the ceiling. The
rays of light passing through the venetian blind gave the office
an almost hallucinatory feeling. Picking up his mail, he sorted
through it: bills from the Chinese restaurant across the street, a
request for an interview from a men's magazine, ads for ladies'
underwear, and a reminder to renew his newspaper subscription
to *Excelsior*.

He wadded it all into a big ball. He wasn't interested in being
interviewed. And *Excelsior* could go screw itself; just look at the
cheap rag it had become.

Using the ball of paper, he dusted off his desk. Not a bad
start to the day. Easygoing, peaceful, quiet. If only it would stay
that way.

From his pocket, he took a photograph of Emiliano Zapata
that he had cut out of an illustrated history of the Mexican
Revolution, and placed it in front of him on the desk. He sat in
silence, contemplating the picture.

An hour later, he turned and, using some tacks stolen from
the upholsterer's toolbox, pinned the picture beside the window
frame. The sad stare of *don* Emiliano followed him as he paced
the room.

The sad stare of Zapata betrayed.

Then he pulled the bag of coins from his jacket pocket, spilling them out onto the desktop, where they jingled and danced,
reflecting bright bits of light as they rolled about.

"May I?"

A woman hesitated in the half-open doorway, looking like
someone out of *Lifestyles of the Rich and Famous*.

"Come on in."

She was about thirty-five years old, and dressed for a different party. Her tight-fitting black pants were tucked into her boot tops, and her see-through black silk blouse sparkled like so many fishing lures. Her long hair was gathered up inside a fine black net. She seemed irrevocably out of place in the squalid office, with its stacks of broken-down furniture and monkey wrenches lying around on the desktops.

"I want to hire you to do a job for me," she said.

Héctor motioned her to take a seat, and stood staring at the strong set of her jaw, the deep glimmer in her eyes.

Taken as a whole, her face seemed better suited to a soft-porn perfume ad than to a friendly conversation.

"Do you recognize me?" she asked, crossing her legs and glancing around the office. She set a black handbag on Héctor's desk.

"I don't watch the soaps," answered Héctor, who was having a hard time taking his eyes off the pair of nipples staring at him through his visitor's blouse.

"My name is Marisa Ferrer…And I want you to keep my daughter from committing suicide…Are you going to just stand there gawking or have you seen enough now?"

"Dressing like that, you must get used to it."

She smiled while Héctor toyed with the coins spread out over the desk.

"I had no idea detectives could be so…"

"Yeah, well, me neither…What's the girl's name?"

"Elena. But don't let yourself be fooled, she's not a child."

"How old is she?"

"Seventeen."

She slid a photograph across the desk.

"What about her father?"

"He owns a hotel chain in Guadalajara. The *Príncipe* chain. They haven't seen each other in seven years, not since we were divorced."

"Does she live with you?"

"Sometimes…Sometimes she lives with her grandmother."

"So what's the story?"

"About two weeks ago she fell from the balcony of her room into the garden. She broke her arm and cut herself on the face. I thought it was an accident. She's very reckless… But then I found this…"

She pulled a stack of photocopies from her handbag and gave them to Héctor. But before he could look them over, she took out another batch of papers. "Then came the second accident," she said, holding out a bundle of newspaper clippings held together with a rubber band. Héctor got the feeling she needed her whole life to be documented in print, corroborated by photographs. Was it just her movie star's obsession, he wondered, a habit garnered somewhere on the long and bitter road to the top?

She produced another photograph, a studio close-up this time, of the girl's face, and then a snapshot, showing her with a big grin and her arm in a cast.

"I don't want her to die," she said.

"Neither do I," answered Héctor, studying the photograph of the smiling girl.

"Will you have dinner with us in my house tomorrow, *Señor* Belascoarán? That way you can get to know Elena." She took an American cigarette from her purse, placed it between her lips, and waited for a chivalrous hand to appear from somewhere and offer her a light.

A ray of bright sunshine slanted across her black blouse.

"Will you take the job, *Señor* Belascoarán?"

The detective found a book of matches and pushed it gently toward her across the desktop, as if it were a toy train maneuvering its way around the coins scattered in its path.

What made her think she could trust him? He wasn't a priest or a psychologist; there wasn't anything fatherly about him. If he understood suicide, it was more through affinity than any objective understanding. He made up his mind, and posted the picture of the smiling girl beside the penetrating eyes of *don* Emiliano.

"In all your things there did you happen to bring your own scrapbook, anything like that?" he asked, already knowing the answer.

She pulled a bulging, leather-bound album from her fathomless handbag.

"Do you think it might help?"

"I couldn't say. But if you're going to give me a bunch of papers to look at, I'd rather have it be a lot than a little. Just personal preference, that's all.... What's for dinner?"

The woman smiled. She got up and turned to leave.

"It's a surprise," she said.

As she opened the door, the bluish light from the hallway filtered into the room and she paused, as if captured in a freeze-frame photo.

"About the money..."

Héctor waved his hand as if to say, don't worry about it, and when the door had closed behind her he turned to face the mountain of papers she'd left for him on his desk. Papers are so much easier to deal with than people, he thought.

Crossing to the wall, he opened up the secret compartment where they kept their valuables: Gilberto's billing receipts, Carlos's hammer, their communal stash of soda pop. He took out a Pepsi-Cola and opened it with his Swiss Army knife.

As he swigged the syrupy liquid, he thought about inflation and what had happened to the price of soda pop. Son of a bitch, he thought. It wasn't so long ago that a Pepsi only cost forty-five cents. *although his actual identity an — mexican can be quetioned*

It was part of what it meant to him to be Mexican, sharing in the general bitching over the rise in prices, the cost of *tortillas*, increases in bus fares, pulling his hair out over the TV news, cursing the police and government corruption. Cursing the whole sad state of affairs, the great national garbage dump that Mexico had become. For Héctor it was a matter of solidarity, of brotherhood, the shared complaints, the shared disgust, the shared pride. Earning the right to call himself *un mexicano*,

*communal bitching against the government, the people*

guarding himself against the curse of starlets like Marisa Ferrer. It kept him in touch with his people.

He paused to give the finger to whoever was responsible for the rising price of soda pop, and returned to his desk with its piles of coins and papers.

The smiling teenager and *don* Emiliano watched him from their respective photographs. In solidarity with Héctor over the price of soft drinks and his giving the finger to the government? Or simply as witnesses to the complicated mess he was stepping into?

Just then the telephone rang.

"Belascoarán Shayne speaking."

"Please wait while I connect you with *Señor* Duelas."

After a brief silence another voice came on the line.

"Hello. *Señor* Shayne?"

"Belascoarán Shayne," Héctor corrected.

"Pardon me, *Señor* Belascoarán Shayne," said the voice, "but one quite naturally tries to avoid your unpronounceable Basque surname."

A vile, honeyed, presumptuous voice.

"If you think that's tough, you should try Belaustiguigoitia, Aurrecoechea, or even Errandoneogoicoechea." Those were the best pseudo-Basque names that came instantly to Héctor's mind.

"Hee hee hee," giggled the voice.

"So what can I do for you?"

"Yes...I'm calling on behalf of the Santa Clara Industrial Council, here in Mexico State. In my capacity as attorney I represent the council in legal matters. We would like to contract your services. Are you available?"

"That all depends, *Señor* Dueñas."

"Duelas."

"Oh, excuse me. Duelas."

"What are your conditions, *Señor* Belascoarán?"

"Like I say, it all depends on what you want me to do."

"On behalf of the council I can send you a report detailing the matter at hand and what we would expect from you. I can arrange to have it to you by early afternoon. As far as money is concerned, we're prepared to offer you a fifteen-day advance, at a rate of one thousand pesos per day. And we're willing to pay you quite generously should you be able to arrange a satisfactory end to our little problem. What do you say, *Señor* Belascoarán?"

Héctor considered the offer for a few seconds. At that point he was interested just to find out what the whole thing was about.

"I'll tell you what, first send me your report, then give me a call at this time tomorrow, and I'll let you know what I think. Okay?"

"Agreed. It's been a pleasure talking with you…"

"Just a second…" he said, turning to glance for permission at the photographs on the wall behind him. "Does this report have any pictures in it?"

"You mean pictures of the body?"

Ah! So there was a body!

"I'd like to have some kind of graphics included in the information you send me."

"Certainly, *Señor* Belascoarán."

"All right, then," said Héctor, and he hung up the phone.

What was he getting himself into? What did he think he was doing taking on three jobs at once? The sweet flame of a temporary insanity tickled his brain, and he smiled, thinking of the old maxim of his pirate father: "*The more complicated the better; the more impossible, the more beautiful.*"

He felt the urge to act, to jump off the edge of the precipice.

Girl with your arm in a cast, *mi general* Emiliano Zapata, the unknown corpse: Héctor Belascoarán Shayne, at your service.

He stashed the old coins in the hidden compartment in the wall, grabbed his jacket, and was about to head for the door. But he stepped over to the phone and dialed the number of the School of Historical Research at the university.

"Dr. Ana Carillo, please…Ana? Could you do me a favor? I need some detailed information on the death of Emiliano Zapata, a couple of books on *Sandinismo*, with pictures, if possible, and something on Rubén Jaramillo. Any chance I can get it by tonight?"

While he waited for the answer, he picked up the note from his office mates and scribbled his reply:

O.K. To post pinup previously censured. Gun w. safety. Don't touch new photo gallery. I suggest we send a letter to congress protesting the high price of soda pop.

—H.B.S.

# Chapter Two

*…I confess that it's easier
for me to explain the things I
reject than the things I want.*

—D. Cohn-Bendit

They sat together like a trio of chastised children in the immense office with its heavy leather furniture, diplomas on the walls, thick carpet, and useless side tables full of equally useless Oriental knickknacks. Héctor looked around unsuccessfully for an ashtray, settling in the end for the bamboo baskets on a small porcelain figure.

"What are we going to do with the house? Where are you going to live?" asked Carlos, gazing out the window at the street six floors below.

"I don't have the slightest idea," answered Elisa.

"Why don't we wait and see what this joker has to tell us, and then we can sit down and talk about it together in peace," suggested Héctor.

And as if Héctor had spoken the magic words, the lawyer appeared, entering through a hidden door in the paneling behind the enormous mahogany desk.

"*Señora, Señores…*" he began ceremoniously.

Elisa and Héctor acknowledged him with a slight nod of the head. Carlos moved his right hand in a short arc, like a politician waving in a parade.

"Would you prefer a full reading of your mother's will at this time, or just a summary of its contents?"

The three of them looked at each other.

"Just the basics would be fine," replied Héctor.

"Well, then…What we have here is your mother's last will and testament, accompanied by a notarized letter addressed to the three of you.

"The letter discusses the origin of the items distributed in the will; it gives a detailed account of the inheritance which she received from her parents in 1957, and the diverse ways in which the inheritance was invested, in various banks and investment firms. It also gives you the information you need to gain access to a safe-deposit box your father left for you upon his death, with the condition that it not be opened during your mother's lifetime…I have the keys to the box, and a letter from your father which gives the three of you the rights to its contents. Finally, your mother's letter gives a complete accounting of all lands and cash monies that she left you."

He paused, before continuing:

"The will is very simple. It's written with a primary clause that takes precedence over the rest. This clause states that the rest of the will be considered null and void if the three of you together are willing to organize the distribution of the estate. In that case, her remaining instructions are to be ignored, although she does ask you to be generous in remembering her longtime servants.

"At this point you need to decide whether you want to take responsibility for distributing the estate yourselves, or if you'd prefer to accept the provisions laid out in the second part of the will. If you want to study the details of the document or discuss it first, you're welcome to do so…"

"There's nothing to discuss," said Elisa.

Her two brothers nodded their heads.

"All right, then, I'll turn over to you a notarized copy of the will, an inventory of the estate, your father's letter and the key to his safe-deposit box, and the letter from your mother. There is, by the way, a second letter from your mother, of a personal nature, with instructions that it be opened in the presence of all three of you."

Elisa took the various items from the lawyer, the last of which was a sealed letter, which she tore open.

"There," she said, "it's been opened in front of the three of us. I suppose that fulfills Mama's wishes."

The lawyer nodded, and the three of them got up to leave.

◇◇◇

He loved to watch the tiny reddish glow of his cigarette in the total darkness. It was strange how not being able to see the smoke made him feel as though he weren't smoking at all. All the same, he could feel the cumulative effect of his habit on his throat and lungs, and for the hundredth time he asked himself if it wouldn't be better to quit once and for all, to say good riddance to the annual bronchitis attack, the taste of copper on his teeth when he woke up in the morning, the craving for tobacco in the middle of the night. He thought about it, shook his head, and went back to staring at the lonely spark of his cigarette in the blackness.

He listened to the approaching steps of his siblings, felt the *click* of the light switch, and closed his eyes. When he opened them again, the room was filled with light.

"You sure you don't want something to eat?" Elisa asked him.

"Na. I've still got a lot of work to do tonight. Were you guys able to make any sense out of it?"

"It wasn't too bad. The lawyer left it all pretty clear. We just inherited somewhere in the neighborhood of a million and a half pesos."

"*Puta madre…*" swore Héctor.

"Can you believe it?" said Elisa. She sat down on the rug, eating a plateful of ham and eggs.

"What are we going to do with it all?"

"Let's burn it…burn it and forget all about it. I was plenty happy without any money up until now," suggested Carlos.

"Me, too," said Héctor.

"Me, three," said Elisa.

"Of course…I'm sure that if we think about it awhile, we'll each be able to come up with about a dozen different things to do with the money."

"No doubt," said Héctor.

"I still can't believe it," said Elisa. "I think that tomorrow it's still going to feel to me like a big joke."

"It's just that…" Carlos began.

"The hell with it," said Héctor.

"Because if we burn it…" interjected Elisa.

"…money corrupts. It's not right to have that much money…" continued Carlos.

It was like in Ecclesiastes: There was a time to sow and a time to reap, a time to keep and a time to throw away. It didn't feel to Héctor like a time to work, there with the black night all around him. But what could he do? Three enormous piles of paper waited for him on his desk.

He crossed to the window and looked down at the street, sad and black, black as coal. A cigarette burned between his lips. The moon was lost behind a pair of clouds, and the streetlights had all gone out. There was a power outage. Far away, the parts of the city that still had power glittered vaguely. A soft, sweet drizzle was falling and Héctor couldn't resist the temptation to open the window, letting the water splash his face and the sound of the rain permeate the room.

"Here's the candles, *amigo*," said a voice at his back.

Héctor turned his head slowly, raindrops dripping from his eyelids, trying to hold on to that vision of the night. What a night for romance, he thought, and with all that work stacked up on his desk.

Three candles shed a furtive light around the office, like a triangle of fire burning in an ancient cave. It made Héctor feel like the Neanderthal Man.

"Got a lot of work tonight?" asked his nocturnal office mate, the infamous engineer, "El Gallo" Villareal, an expert on Mexico City's sewer system who sublet the plumber's portion of the office at night.

Héctor stared at him fixedly for a moment: he couldn't have been more than twenty-five years old, with a bushy mustache, jeans and cowboy boots, and a heavy jacket that he always wore draped over his shoulders. He sat permanently hunched over his maps, except when he went out on his strange, subterranean explorations of the city's sewer system. A yellow hard hat with a headlamp, a pair of asbestos gloves, and a pair of fire fighter's thick rubber boots occupied a chair beside his drawing table.

In the flickering candlelight he looked like an ancient alchemist puzzling over the riddle of the philosopher's stone.

El Gallo looked up from his maps and stared inquisitively at the detective who stood in dark profile in front of one of the winking candles.

"How did you get started in this stuff?" asked the detective.

"You know how it is, neighbor, shit happens. That's life." He searched through his jacket pockets for one of his small, thin cigars. "You think I don't get excited about my work, is that it?"

Héctor nodded.

"Did you see *The Phantom of the Opera* when you were a kid?"

Héctor nodded.

"I suppose it never occurred to you that the single basic difference between a city of the Middle Ages and today's capitalist city is the modern sewer system."

Héctor shook his head.

"Hell, I'll bet that it never even occurred to you that someday you could wake up floating in shit up to your eyeballs if there wasn't somebody out there making sure it didn't happen…I've seen your kind before—you're the kind of guy who shits and forgets, the kind of guy who never thinks about where his shit is going."

Héctor nodded.

"You hate technocrats, don't you? Engineers, scientists…"

Héctor nodded.

"Well, so do I. I couldn't care less if the whole damn city filled up with shit—more than it is already, I mean. I couldn't give a flying fuck if the whole damn sewer system all the way from the Miramontes Canal to the Deep Drainage Network fills up with crap!"

Héctor nodded, a smile stealing across his face.

"The deal is that I get two thousand pesos for every one of these maps that I analyze. You know, for capacity, resistance, that kind of thing…It's a living, what can I say…?" He lit a cigar.

"And I'll tell you something else. If you've got to spend your life making a living at something, you might as well do your best to glamorize it a little. You know, I try to think about the Phantom of the Opera living in the sewers in Paris, or that movie about the Polish Resistance in World War II, where they had this whole battle down in the stinking sewer. You've got to find a way to care about what you're doing, that's all I'm trying to say."

"Look, I used to be an engineer, too. I was an Efficiency Expert, if you can believe it," Héctor began. But he balked at the thought of dredging up the not-so-distant past, and returned to his desk before he went on. "And you know what? There are some jobs that they can just take and stick up their ass."

"I hear you." The sewer specialist and expert in fecal flooding nodded.

El Gallo Villareal started humming the victory march from the opera *Aïda*, as if they'd been talking about nothing more than the weather, or the power outage, or the blackness of the night.

Belascoarán took his seat in front of the pile of reports, and reached for the closest one.

The oscillating candlelight flickered rhythmically across the page in front of him. He felt a promise in the night.

# Chapter Three

## In Which Héctor Studies
## The Three Case Files:

A teenager's diary and a supposed suicide attempt; the still-warm body of a murdered engineer; and a hero from the past who threatens to rise up from the grave.

It is necessary to follow the trail throughout the night.

—Paco Urondo ~~s~~ *argentinian poet killed by dictatorship*

The investigation should ~~take each detail of the material into account.~~

—Marx

*should appropriate the matter in all of its detail*

*(better translation from spanish)*

Héctor spread the material from the first stack out in front of him: the photocopied pages of a diary, filled with an irregular scrawl; a small bundle of newspaper reports about the second "accident," held together with a rubber band; two photographs, one a typical studio portrait, the other a snapshot showing a smiling girl dressed in a school uniform; and a leather-bound scrapbook full of newspaper clippings.

He lit a cigarette and singled out the second photo, placing his hands closely around it in a protective gesture. He was touched by what he saw.

In the background, the door to the school could be seen, slightly out of focus; a man selling sweets from a cart stood with his back to the camera, while three girls walked arm in arm across one of the upper corners. A traffic cop occupied the opposite corner of the picture. In the center stood a seventeen-year-old girl in a white blouse, plaid skirt, and knee socks. She had lively, alert eyes and hair that fell thickly over her shoulders, a medium complexion, and a wide forehead. There was an air about her that was very reminiscent of her mother, hard to put a finger on exactly, but unmistakable all the same.

In the studio close-up, the characteristics of adolescence had begun to disappear from her face. The overall impression was of a young woman, who, if not beautiful, was quite pretty, likeable, and something more.

He considered whether to turn next to the girl's diary or her mother's scrapbook. Finally, he chose the scrapbook. He wanted some kind of context to fit it all into, sensing that there was something more to the affair than a simple case of attempted suicide.

Marisa Ferrer's scrapbook contained an illustrated history of her career, one actress's sad trajectory from oblivion to stardom, Mexican style.

The story started with a series of small clippings from provincial newspapers, mostly from Guadalajara, with a name underlined in red pencil, always at the very end of the article.

At that time she still used her full name: Marisa Andrea González Ferrer. All of her roles were small ones in student productions, and there was no mention of her individual performance or abilities. Finally she landed a small part in a play by Lorca. The clipping included a grainy, faded photo, in which he could barely make out a skinny girl in the background, dressed in black, with arms outstretched.

Next, there was a brief commentary on her performance of a minor role in a commercial production, *One Husband for Three Sisters*. This was followed by a dormant period that lasted six months, only to be broken by three spectacular full-page magazine photos in which the skinny girl reappeared as a svelte woman in a bikini, captioned: "ALL THE INGREDIENTS FOR SUCCESS". It was followed by an interview in which neither the interviewer nor his subject had anything much to say. The last question was meant to be funny: REPORTER: "And what about men?" WOMAN IN BIKINI: "For right now they don't enter into my plans. I'm not interested in men…They just get in the way of your career." Next came two pages of cinema listings, with a pair of movies underlined in red, in which she apparently had some bit part too small to get her name in the credits: *The Hour of the Wolf*, and *Strange Companions*. According to the promotion, the first was a movie about professional wrestlers, and the second a teen romance. After that her picture started to appear in some of the magazines from around Mexico City.

The quantity of her clothing diminished with each successive appearance. She shortened her name, discarding the Andrea and the González, and the size of the print increased by ten points; she allowed a glimpse of her left breast in front of the camera, and the size of her panties grew progressively scantier. Learning to sing passably well, she made the night-club circuit, and recorded an album of *rancheras*, showing up eventually in the gossip columns as the current companion to the owner of a recording studio. Shortly thereafter, she displayed her naked backside for a photo session in *Audaz*, and then won her first starring role in a feature film.

Thirteen glowing reviews in a single week testified to her success. It was followed by her first all-nude spread in a trendy skin-mag, accompanied by a lively interview. Héctor took note of some of her answers: "In this business, war is war, the army with the best guns wins…" "Loneliness? What's that? There's never any time to feel lonely…" "I don't like to have to pose naked for very long. The photographers never pay any attention to the heating and it's too easy to catch cold…" "I like what I'm doing."

He was halfway through the album before he stopped. Where was the daughter?

Calculating that if she was seventeen years old today, she would have been born in 1960, he thumbed back through the album, scrutinizing the clippings more carefully until he got to the blank space of six months way back at the start of her mother's career. Apparently the actress had pursued her career and raised the child all at the same time.

Figuring he'd gotten the basic idea, he closed the heavy book. If he had to look at any more pictures of his client in the nude, he was going to get all caught up in her naked breasts, her smooth buttocks, and never be able to look at her again with her clothes on.

On the other side of the room, El Gallo was still hunched over his maps, taking notes. Belascoarán walked to the hidden cupboard and took out a soda pop.

"I'll have one, thanks," said the engineer, without looking up from his work.

Héctor got out another tamarind soda and used the upholsterer's scissors to pry the tops off both the bottles.

Returning to his desk, he took up the girl's diary, glancing first at the smiling face in the photo, as if to apologize for invading her privacy.

The photocopied portion was only a small section of the original diary. It started on page 106 and ended on page 114. The handwriting was careful and elegant, as if taken from a calligraphy manual, and appeared to have been written entirely with the same fountain pen. It looked like a typical teen diary, jealously guarded under a pillow, or hidden in a bottom desk drawer under a mountain of old papers, where nobody else would ever look, to be removed from its hiding place every night before bed, and receive the secret thoughts and feelings of its young owner.

The entries, separated from one another by a pair of minute crosses, were each very brief. Some of them were in code, giving Héctor the impression he was dealing with some indecipherable children's game. There were no dates, although sometimes a day of the week was mentioned.

> I can't keep taking it all the time, holding it in. Never saying anything. It's like they just threw me into the water and said: Go ahead, bitch, swim.

> What should I do? What's going to happen? There's nothing to do but wait.

> Read p. 105 for Thursday.

> That stupid history teacher. What a conceited pimp. I wish I could tell him how much I hate him. He's got that stupid tic, I wonder if he even knows it. I'm sure he's impotent and he probably has the hots for his own mother. Ever since he was a little kid, I bet. Besides which, he doesn't know a damn thing about history!

> I don't think Mama knows that I know. How can I keep her from finding out? I'm such an idiot. What should I do? I just spent the whole day bouncing

back and forth around the house like a stupid ball. If I keep up like this she's bound to suspect something. I've got to just pretend like everything's normal, go to school, go to the movies, find a new boyfriend, read books...

G. says 35 grand. Maybe I'd better ask someone else.

I think I just don't know how to fall in love.

Books I want to read: *Justine, The Misadventures of a Stewardess, Desire and Destiny.*

Gisela says she has a copy. Remember to tell Carolina and Bustamante.

G. is adamant. Just to see his reaction I told him sixty. He didn't seem surprised.

I want to live somewhere else. Have a different room. I don't like the same things I used to. I don't like rum raisin ice cream. I don't like Arturo's kisses. I don't like cars, I don't like to go to the movies. It's just something about me, it doesn't have anything to do with all these other things.

And in the middle of this mess, what do I do? Start reading a biography of Van Gogh.

G.'s putting on the pressure. He introduced me to Es. I didn't like him at all, he gave me the creeps.

Ay, Mama, Mama, what's wrong with you? How come you don't notice what's going on? There was almost a fight between Bustamante's boyfriend, another friend of his, and Es. They saw him threaten me when I came out of school. But I told them to stay out of it.

There's no point in saying anything to them. It's true, they acted like good boys, but I still don't trust them. They're a couple of fools, really. Afterwards they went around like big heroes, telling everyone they saved my life.

There's no one I can turn to.

I guess the days of bobby sox and miniskirts are over. Maybe they can help me get a gun.

I'm afraid.

I'm flunking English and sociology.

Mama, I swear to you that I'm trying to stay alive, to do everything I'm supposed to. You don't understand what's going on. I want everything to be OK. But it's all happening too fast, Mama. It's like in that movie we saw a few months ago, with the guy who says, "Life is too big for me."

I flunked history. That asshole!

I've been crying all afternoon. I'm not a little girl anymore. I've got to find a way to stand up to them. I've got to do something. Maybe I could run away. Where would I go? Who could I go with? With all of the friends I've had over the last couple of years, who do I have left now? Nobody. Nobody.

What can I do? As if I knew how to do anything.

They say they'll give me 40 thousand pesos. But I know they're lying. They're trying to trick me.

Arturo broke up with me. When I told Mama she yelled at me like she's never done before. At school everybody stares at me. They've all seen G.'s friends waiting for me outside.

I spend all my time shut up here in my room. I hate it here.

If I get out of this mess, I'm going to paint my room a different color. But I'm not going to get out of it. They're going to get me.

And I'm only seventeen years old.

They're going to kill me. I wish I'd never started this thing.

That was all. Belascoarán wished the mother had given him the diary in its entirety. He felt an enormous compassion for the girl smiling at him from the photo, with her arm in a cast. If he had kept a diary himself he would have written something like: "Paternal instincts aroused. They need me. I feel useful. I can help them. Leave off eating shit for a while, and go save the maiden in distress. Life is good when you can help someone. Time to sharpen your .45, noble knight. Belascoarán to the rescue!"

But since he wasn't prone to that sort of thing, he limited himself to a few notes in the margins of the diary.

Then he pulled the rubber band from the small bundle of newspaper clippings. They all told the same story, illustrated with photographs, of the near-disastrous failure of an apartment building elevator.

The springs in the basement and a lucky stop at the third floor miraculously saved the life of the elevator's only occupant. "After two hours of rescue efforts the young woman emerged from the wreckage shaken but unharmed." "Company experts are now investigating the failure of the safety mechanisms."

Who would try to commit suicide by sabotaging an elevator?

Across the room, the engineer shuffled his maps, then relit a candle extinguished by the sudden movement of air.

"How's it going?"

"So so," answered the detective, declining the cigar El Gallo offered him. He took out his pack of Delicado filters and lit a cigarette. He could feel his shell softening and the long-forgotten anxieties of adolescence pulsing again through his veins. It was the strangest feeling. Maybe it would have seemed more normal a few years ago. But by now, he would have thought that he was far enough from adolescence to preserve some kind of distance. Not so.

What a profession, he thought. What a wonderful job this is. But he was ashamed to think of the poor girl, unable to sleep, all alone, just seventeen and already mixed up in who knows what kind of trouble.

He yawned. What next? he wondered. Nothing to do but forge ahead, dive on into the two other worlds still waiting for his attention. New and totally different. Separate. In your typical mystery novel everything always fits so neatly together. But what in the hell could a confused teenager possibly have in common with the Santa Clara Industrial Council, and the ghost of Emiliano Zapata? A lot of nothing, that's what.

"You a soccer fan?" asked his office mate.

"No, why?"

"Oh, no reason, I just wondered."

Héctor opened the packet the lawyer, *Señor* Duelas, had sent him.

It consisted of a series of documents from the public prosecutor's office, police reports, and newspaper clippings. At the end were seven pages of signed testimony, each one typed on a different machine and a different kind of paper. All together, they told the story of a murder.

What does a detective do when he needs to change gears? Is it enough to just turn the page and go on?

Héctor considered it for a moment and then went out to take a piss. The bathroom was at the end of the hall. He groped his way through the darkened building, past doorways, stairwell, the service elevator, the passenger elevator, and finally the door to the men's room. He pushed it, but it was locked. And of course, he never had his keys when he needed them. So he used the women's bathroom instead. It was uncharted territory in the dark, and he walked smack into one of the sinks.

Guiding himself by the sound of the piss in the bowl, he adjusted his aim until the stream fell directly into the water at the center. When he finished, he shook it off, sprinkling the last drops onto his pants in the darkness.

He retraced his steps through the blackened hallway to the candlelit office, where the open file waited for him on his desk. He looked at his watch: 3:17 in the morning.

The old chair complained under his weight.

"Tired, neighbor?" asked El Gallo.

"No, just getting my second wind. It's been a while."

Héctor sank his gaze into the papers on his desk. As he read, he pieced the information together into a kind of Mexican police story, the sort of thing you could read in the newspaper any day of the week.

RADIO CAR GOT THE CALL AT 6:20 P.M.

Patrol cars 118 and 76 of the Tlanepantla Police Department reported to the corner of Avenida Morelos and Carlos B. Zetina, where the head office and factory of the Delex Steel Corporation are located. They were met by plant supervisor Zenón Calzada, who directed them to the office where the body was found.

I SAW THE BODY THROUGH THE OPEN DOOR.

The janitor, Gerónimo Barrientos, discovered the body twenty minutes earlier. The office would normally have been empty at that time.

THE BODY LAY SPRAWLED ACROSS THE DESK.

Black leather shoes, black socks. A light gray suit of good quality, tailor-made. Red tie, with gray stripes, soaked with blood. He fell so that his face lay in the cigarette butts in a heavy metal ashtray, cast in the shape of a foundry mold, on his desk. The window was open. His feet were suspended a few inches above the floor in an unnatural position. His hands appeared open and relaxed, palms facing outward, arms at his sides. His broken glasses were found under the body.

ACCORDING TO HIS SECRETARY:

Nothing was out of place. Everything in order. "Just like always."

SHE LEFT THE OFFICE AT 4:30:

Half an hour earlier than usual, but only because her boss told her she could go early, and that he was expecting someone, and yes, it's true, she always stayed at least until five o'clock, and usually later because she was normally the one who locked up the office at the end of the day, but this time she left early because her boss told her to, and if they want to ask someone just talk to Guzmán Vera, the accountant, who was sitting right on her desk eating a doughnut when the engineer called her on the intercom.

What was that? Who was he waiting for? No, he didn't say. Who knows who it was? she said.

THE THIRD BLOW PIERCED THE HEART:

Two other deep incisions were made with the same sharp, pointed object; the first punctured his left lung, the second also struck the heart.

Death was instantaneous. Within two or three seconds, at the most.

SOMETHING IS ALWAYS MISSING:

It's the picture of his ex-wife that he always kept there on his desk. Where he fell he would have been lying right on top of it, and so I didn't notice until later that it was gone.

The murder weapon—kitchen knife? dagger? bayonet? letter opener?—was also missing.

FINGERPRINTS?

"We could spend months sorting through the fingerprints of all the different people that have been inside this office. Forget it," said the lab specialist.

And finally, the photograph. Héctor picked it up and studied it carefully. The body seemed somehow to be hiding, as though it were actually fading away under the influence of death. He found it disconcerting, the way it lay there in that strange position, slumped over the desk, arms at its sides and the palms of the hands facing outward. It lacked a certain seriousness appropriate to death. But who said death had to be serious?

There were three pictures in all. The second one showed the face of a man about forty years old, with a few gray hairs creeping in at the sides, a faint mustache, and a penetrating, humorless expression.

The other picture showed the same man inside a factory, gesturing toward an enormous industrial oven as he spoke to a small group of people, among whom Héctor recognized the governor of the state of Mexico.

After thinking about it for several minutes, he chose the photo of the dead body, and went over to steal four more tacks from the upholsterer's toolbox. Zapata and the girl with her arm in the cast watched as he added the new arrival to the small photo gallery on the wall.

"Aren't you going to put up a picture of the Virgin of Guadalupe, too?" asked El Gallo, without looking up from his maps.

"The deceased was a colleague of yours, Gallo."

"My colleagues can go fuck themselves," the engineer answered dryly. Putting down his pencil, he looked up at the detective and smiled broadly from under his big mustache.

The very least that could be said about Héctor's corner of the room was that it was taking on a surrealistic character. The detective turned back to the papers in front of him.

PROFILE OF A DEAD ENGINEER.

GASPAR ALVAREZ CERRULI was born in Guadalajara in 1936. He received a bachelor's degree in industrial engineering from Jalisco Tech, and a master's in personnel management at Iowa State University. From 1966 to 1969 he worked in the *maquiladoras*, or sweatshops, for various Mexican-American companies in Mexicali and Tijuana. In 1970 he became the personnel manager for the Delex consortium, and in 1974, he was made assistant manager of their Santa Clara plant.

He also held a 42-percent share in the Trinidad Mattress Company, which was managed by his brother. Married in 1973, divorced in 1975, no children.

THE POLICE INTERROGATED THE COMPANY EMPLOYEES:

But nobody knew anything. The shifts were changing in the factory, and the office workers had gone home at least an hour before. Everyone was milling around the yard, or in the locker rooms. The two shift supervisors, Fernández from personnel and engineer Camposanto, were inside the plant drinking coffee. They preferred the coffee from Fernández's thermos to the brew from the office vending machine, which was only a few yards from the door to the room where the murder took place. "Just imagine if we had gone to get some coffee from the machine…"

ALL THE SAME, NO ONE UNUSUAL WAS SEEN GOING IN OR OUT.

Reported gatekeeper and security guard Rubio, badge number 6453. There were two trucks from Eagle Scrap Iron and a bill collector from Electra earlier in the day, but they all left before 4:30. Everyone else is listed here in the register, and they're all company employees. There's no possibility of any mistake. Everybody punches in and out, except, of course, *Señor* Rodríguez Cuesta, the company president, but I specifically remember when he left because he asked me to have his car jack fixed for him.

THAT LIMITS THE POSSIBLE SUSPECTS TO:

The three hundred twenty seven workers on this list.

FOR YOUR EYES ONLY, FROM SEÑOR DUELAS:

"*Señor* Belascoarán, it should be noted that the deceased was not a popular man. He was reserved, and prone to violent outbursts. Although very professional in his work, he did not get along well with people. I am including a list of the workers who are still employed by Delex, and who had serious run-ins with the deceased during his tenure as personnel manager for the company. (There followed a list with sixty-one names, of whom twenty-seven were in the factory at the time of the murder.)

"In case you're interested, I have also included some information about the corporation, its directors, and its financial standing. The information is quite general, but I doubt you'll need to probe any deeper."

RANDOM DETAILS OF POTENTIAL SIGNIFICANCE:

a) No one attended the funeral.
b) The ex-wife's address: Number 57 Cerro dos Aguas, in the Pedregal neighborhood.
c) The dead man's salary: thirty two thousand pesos per month.
d) The investigation is to be made under the auspices of the Industrial Council; it was requested by Rodríguez Cuesta, president of Delex, who will cover the costs personally.
e) A similar murder occurred two months earlier at the Nalgion-Reyes chemical plant. The victim was an engineer named Osorio Barba.
f) The Delex factory in Santa Clara is currently targeted for a strike by the Independent Union of Iron and Steel Workers and Related Trades of the Republic of Mexico. There is a second, nominal union operating at the plant, which the company characterizes as "very cooperative."
g) The deceased's maid can still be found at his home: 2012 Luz Saviñón. She has instructions to let the detective inside. The house is assumed to be the property of the dead man's brother, at least for the time being.
h) Parents are dead. He didn't belong to any club or professional association. He didn't subscribe to any newspaper.

Getting up from his desk, Héctor crossed to the window and lit a cigarette. Nothing moved in the darkened street below.

"How long's it been since the lights went out?"

El Gallo checked his watch in the candlelight. "A little over two hours."

Héctor opened the window, and the candle flames danced in the breeze. The heavy scent of the city and the interminable night rushed into the room. Yawning, Héctor stared out at the buildings, the parked cars, the darkened lampposts, the black windows.

He felt a certain uneasiness. The old inertia had taken hold of him once again, throwing him full force into other people's lives. Like a ghost, he walked through strange worlds. Wasn't that, after all, what being a detective was all about? Too afraid to really live his own life, to commit himself once and for all, unequivocally, to a life inside the skin that he was born into? Living for others was an excuse, a vicarious life. And now, the inertia following his mama's death. And the emptiness of living in a country that he didn't understand, but that he longed to experience with intensity. Together these things propelled him into the strange chaos where he found himself now. Was it going to go on like that forever? No, it wasn't possible. Someday he'd find himself standing in front of a door with his own name on it.

But in the meantime, he greeted his clients with an impassive stare, an impenetrable mask that occasionally showed signs of intelligence, moments of humor, or strength, hiding, all the while, an overwhelming sense of surprise, of astonishment at the world around him.

"What a mess," he complained. Reserving his right as a Mexican to bitch as a last resort. It was the solution *par excellence* for all of life's problems.

"Couldn't have said it better myself," agreed the sewer engineer. "What a mess."

Belascoarán returned to his desk and opened the third bundle, a folder, a pair of books, and several photocopied pages.

The information his friend Ana had sent him was clear and concise, and Héctor quickly distilled a brief summary of the relevant facts.

The story that Zapata had not died on the ranch in Chinameca was an old one. It held a great deal of currency in the years following his assassination, and despite its many versions always contained some element of apparent fact to give it greater legitimacy. Some of the most common versions were:

a) The real Zapata had once lost a finger when a pistol exploded in his hand. The body at Chinameca had all ten fingers.

b) The version Héctor had already heard, that Zapata had a *compaño who looked a lot like him.*

c) The story that Zapata's horse didn't recognize the body. His horse was said to have loved him tremendously.

d) *Don* Emiliano had both a mark on his chest and a wart on his right cheek. The corpse at Chinameca had neither.

The rumors circulated in the newspapers of the period, and the government did its best to eradicate them. A film of the body, taken in the plaza in Celaya, was distributed, along with a series of photographs in which the flies hovered thickly over the corpse.

In recent years, social anthropologists had been busy recording the myriad stories involving the survival of Zapata. One bizarre version that surfaced now and then had *don* Emiliano escaping from Morelos with a band of Arab merchants whom he traveled around the world with, selling cloth.

Belascoarán shook his head wearily. It was no good. There was nothing consistent. Just wild rumors produced in desperation by a people deprived of their leader; it was a natural defense against an enemy that controlled both media and myth.

Patiently, he scrutinized the pictures included in the books on Sandinismo. Only in one did he see the glimpse of a possibility: in the foreground, General Sandino with his lieutenants, faces sunk in shadow beneath their wide-brimmed hats. Agustín Farabundo Martí smiling behind a thick mustache, the Honduran general Porfirio Sánchez, the Guatemalan general María Manuel Girón Ramos. And in the background, a dark face, a small, clipped mustache, eyes completely hidden beneath his hat brim: "Captain Zenón Enríquez, Mexican," read the caption.

It was the only clue he could find.

If the cases of the Ferrer girl and the murdered engineer seemed at first glance to be extraordinarily complex, at least they made some sense, at least he had some idea of where to start, which leads to follow; but this craziness about Emiliano Zapata seemed to have neither beginning nor end.

Raising his tired eyes, he looked to the three photos on the wall for inspiration, as if they might offer him some clue.

He set the material on Zapata's old *compañero* Rubén Jaramillo aside, promising himself that he'd finish it tomorrow. Then, extinguishing the candles on his desk, he got up and headed straight for the old leather armchair where he sometimes slept.

"Time for bed, neighbor?"

"Time for a little snooze," answered Héctor. "Say there, Engineer, how late do you work anyway?"

"Oh, until about six, Ex-engineer."

Héctor lowered himself into the armchair and wrapped his gabardine coat around himself. He lit a cigarette and watched the first mouthful of smoke float lazily up toward the ceiling where shadows danced in the candlelight. He shut his eyes.

"What are you working on now?" he asked.

"Oh, nothing much. I'm just checking to see if another heavy rain like the one we had yesterday could overload the network in the Northeast…and leave everybody in Lindavista knee-deep in a lake of piss."

"Man, I love this city. It's magical, you know? I mean, where else? You never know what crazy-ass son-of-a-bitching kind of thing is going to happen next…"

"I'll bet you didn't talk like that when you were an engineer," said El Gallo.

"That's just part of the magic," answered Héctor.

# Chapter Four

It's better to light a candle
than to curse the darkness.

—Roberto Fernández Retamar

"Milkman time," his sister used to call it years ago when they walked together to school in the early morning, long before the sun dared to show its face. Even at that early hour the streets would be thronged with people. Now, Héctor left the office with El Gallo and they walked down to the corner, where the sewer expert said good-bye and disappeared into the fog. The cold oppressed Héctor; the cold, and the fact that he'd slept for barely two hours. The streetlights had come back on again, after the night-long blackout. Héctor lit a cigarette and walked with a brisk step, trying to guess the occupations of the men who huddled at the street corners waiting for their buses.

That one's a teacher; that one there's a builder; that one's a laborer; that one, a student; that one, a butcher's helper; that one's a reporter going home to sleep. That one looks like a detective, he thought, catching his own reflection in a store window. The blackness of the night began to give way to a grayish false dawn.

As the light changed, the street noise stepped up its violent pitch. Héctor paused in front of a mirror outside a drugstore, and examined the dark bags under his eyes. His pupils were two bright points of light. He felt good, in spite of his fatigue and the cold. It was the city, the city he loved so intensely, so selflessly, welcoming him with that dirty gray dawn. And more than the city, even more, it was the people.

Maybe what had happened was that the combination of the cold and the hostile dawn had awakened people to a sense of their common humanity. Already he'd run across six smiling faces in the six blocks he'd covered so far. It was the kind of smile you give away early on a cold morning, to the first stranger you see.

He squeezed onto an Artes-Pino bus bound for the Refinería. In the crush of commuters, he held his arm to his side, trying to hide the gun in its shoulder holster, but it was all he could do to keep from mashing gun, holster, arm and all, in a secretary's face, while trying simultaneously to dislodge someone else's briefcase from his asshole and dodge a large T-square that threatened to knock his teeth out at the first sudden stop.

He got out at Artes and walked along Sadi Carnot in the direction of the school. Small groups of girls stood here and there in the street, and by the time he was half a block away, the sounds of traffic were drowned out by the happy chatter of young voices. He stopped across from the school entrance, next to a cart of steaming tamales, and propped himself up against a wall to wait. The heat rising from the tamale cart made him even sleepier than he had been before.

A group of girls stood talking on the steps, gesturing dramatically with their hands, taking advantage of the last few minutes left before the start of another day in "jail." Now and then, an incredibly nearsighted young nun would appear in the doorway, with the sole intention of showing herself to the dawdlers outside.

It was a quarter to seven, and already the dawn, its clean light struggling against the gray, seemed to have the upper hand.

A pale green Rambler wagon pulled up a few yards past Héctor, and two young men got out. They opened the back of the station wagon, took out two bottles from a full case of soda pop, and pried off the tops with a screwdriver.

Héctor saw what he was waiting for at a distance. She walked with a hurried step, her arm still in a cast, and with a purple ribbon hung around her shoulder as a sling. Her uniform beret was cocked to one side of her head, and the long plaid skirt billowed around her as she walked. Under her good arm, she carried an awkward load of books; a gray bag hung from her shoulder. Her face was serious, and her hurried manner was reflected in the lines that wrinkled her forehead. Héctor let her walk past him without moving. Suddenly, the two youths left the Rambler and walked toward the girl, blocking her path before she could cross the street. She raised her eyes and stared at them in surprise. One of the boys threw his pop bottle to the ground, and it exploded at her feet, scattering shards of glass across the sidewalk. The other boy stood directly in front of her and grabbed her good arm. Her load of books fell to the ground.

Héctor unglued himself from the wall as the first boy took the pop bottle out of his partner's hand, and crashed it down in front of the girl. Bits of broken glass flew through the air.

The tamale seller left his cart and followed after the detective.

Out of the corner of his eye, Héctor saw a third boy get out of the station wagon, carrying three more bottles in his hands.

The terrified girl struggled wordlessly to free herself from her attackers, without making a sound, like a character from a silent movie.

"Game's over," said Héctor as he reached them.

"Mind your own business," growled one of the youths. He wore a green corduroy jacket over a dark red sweater. He was tall, with chestnut hair, and a small scar under his right eye.

That's where Héctor aimed his first blow, a backhanded slap that sent the boy reeling backward. Then he turned and kicked the other boy in the calf. The boy shouted in pain, let go of the girl's arm, and fell to the ground, on top of the broken glass.

The third youth was stopped short by the tamale seller, who brandished an iron bar that he'd pulled from who knew where.

Greenjacket took the screwdriver from his pocket.

"Who asked you to butt in, asshole?" scowled his partner.

"The archangel Gabriel," answered Héctor, glancing at the sister who watched the scene in surprise from the school steps.

Then he kicked him in the chin. He could hear the jawbone crack.

It was this way of attacking unexpectedly, and without warning, that made it possible for Héctor to keep control of the situation. He stood casually, with one hand in his pocket, not looking at the others, but staring absentmindedly at the books scattered across the pavement. Then suddenly, out of nowhere, he kicked the kid in the face.

Greenjacket backed away. "What'd you have to kick him for?" he whined.

"I'm an asshole, what can I say? Life's rough," Héctor answered, and without thinking, he took out his gun and shot into the case of soda pop in the back of the Rambler. The bottles burst, spilling their dark liquid onto the street. Three late-arriving students ran shrieking into the school.

The three young thugs made a break for their car.

Greenjacket clutched the screwdriver and Armgrabber held his chin in one hand, spitting blood.

Héctor stowed the gun in his jacket pocket and turned to smile at the tamale man.

"It was a lucky shot," he confessed. "Normally I can't hit a thing at this distance."

The tamale man smiled back at Héctor and returned to his cart. The Rambler lurched into reverse and raced backwards all the way to the end of the block.

The girl gathered her books from the sidewalk, watching Héctor with a mixture of admiration and astonishment.

"Who are you?" she asked him, taking a step toward the safety of the school yard.

"My name's Belascoarán," mumbled Héctor, staring at the ground and crushing little bits of glass under his toe.

"Belascoar*án*, my guardi*an*." She laughed, taking another step in the direction of the school.

"Belascoarán Shayne," he said, raising his eyes to look at the girl. "What time do you get out of school?"

"Two," she said, and stopped.

"Wait for me here. I might be late." He shoved his hands down into his pants pockets and walked slowly away, without waiting for an answer, and without looking back. The girl watched him for a second, and then turned and ran up the steps to the school. A nun waited for her in the doorway, and she took the girl into her arms and hugged her tightly.

The man with the tamale cart watched Héctor disappear down the block.

He caught a North Freeway bus at the Monument to the Revolution and rode standing, holding on to the bar with his right hand. The back of his left hand hurt and it was turning red. At Avenida Hidalgo he changed his mind and got off the bus, sorting his way through the mass of people coming and going from the Mexico City headquarters of the ruling Institutional Revolutionary Party, until he got to one of the used-book stores that lined the avenue. If he was going to spend the whole morning on a bus, he wanted to have something to read. He rummaged for a while through a pile of old books, until he picked out a well-thumbed copy of Dos Passos's *Manhattan Transfer*. Inside the torn front cover someone had written: To Joaquin, from Laura Flores P., with love. Héctor haggled the price down to eight pesos and paid for the book.

Then he got onto another North Freeway bus and found a seat in back, where he rode as far as Rancho del Charro. He read a couple of chapters, taking time out now and then to notice what a dump the north end of town had become since his student days, when he used to go on geology field trips all the way up to Indios Verdes.

A great big smile spread across his face every time he thought about the fight.

He wasn't a violent man. He never had been, having managed more or less to survive the violence that surrounded him without getting involved, like a spectator watching from a distance. He couldn't remember more than maybe a couple of fights toward the end of his university days, and then one fight years later, in a movie theater, when some guy tried to snatch his ex-wife's purse. In that one, he'd come out the worse by far, with a split lip after the guy hit him with an umbrella. In the end, it was the style of the fighting rather than the actual result that interested him the most. His own style was dry, cold, detached. And now, every time the pain in his hand reminded him of the morning's fight, he smiled, until he finally felt embarrassed by the amount of childish pleasure he got out of the incident. At Indios Verdes he transferred to a green San Pedro–Santa Clara bus, and read another whole chapter as the vehicle lurched its way slowly through the industrial suburb of Xalostoc, dodging potholes and menacing cyclists. Pulling the cord, he descended the steps and, holding on to the handrail, leaned out of the moving bus, with the wind rushing across his face. At Brenner Street he jumped off. A light rain was falling.

It wasn't as though he'd never been there before. Twice a day for four long years he'd driven that same stretch of highway, with his eyes fixed on the road ahead of him, hating the dust, the open-air market, the never-ending road work, and the masses of men that stormed the buses at five-thirty every afternoon. He'd tried to ignore it all, driving home in the evening toward the comfortable security of his nauseatingly middle-class neighborhood, trying not to let himself be distracted by the multitude of things he half-felt, guessed at, intuited. Trying to separate himself from that industrial wasteland raised up amidst the dust and the misery of one hundred thousand new immigrants from the countryside, the sulphurous puddles, the air thick with dust, the drunken cops, the rampant land fraud, the illegal slaughter of infected cattle, the sub-minimum wages, the cold that rides in on the east wind, the unemployment.

Out there, modern industry took a step backward into the nineteenth century, to the days before the invention of hard hats, to the era of rusty steel, lost time sheets, cheap raw materials, and thieving bosses who stole with impunity from the workers' savings accounts. There in Santa Clara the intrinsic filth of Mexican capital, in other places hidden behind white-washed walls and hygienic facades, was laid open for all to see.

But, for all the time Belascoarán had spent there, he knew he'd barely even scratched the surface, never really wanting to see any more. At the end of every day his car waited for him at the factory gate, and he drove the next three miles without ever leaving the main road, with his windows rolled up and the stereo on.

His eyes and ears had been closed.

Now, as he got off the bus, he was filled with a vague feeling of guilt, and he made a beeline for a roadside juice stand where four or five workers stood finishing their breakfast.

"Orange juice, please."

"You want an egg in it?"

The combination had never appealed much to Héctor.

"Plain is fine."

He took the glass of juice, but his eyes were on the cloud of dust disappearing down the highway.

The workers moved to one side to make room for Héctor, who picked up scattered bits of their conversation. Something about somebody's fat ass, a foreman's pimply face, and a quack government doctor who recommended aspirin for rheumatic attacks. It all mixed together in Héctor's mind.

He paid for the juice, and ventured a weak smile in the direction of the workers. They ignored him. He made his way on foot farther into the industrial zone.

"Go ahead, boss," said the security guard at the gate.

Héctor committed the man's face to memory.

The inner courtyards were painted a lead gray, in sharp contrast to the blue outer wall covered with red graffiti: DOWN WITH LIRA. BETTER WAGES OR STRIKE. DOWN WITH DOG ZENÓN. STRIKE…

Behind the gatekeeper stood a pair of especially tough-looking guards, one of whom carried a sawed-off double-barreled shotgun under his arm.

Héctor guided himself through the maze of buildings, courtyards, and walkways, ending up at the large, high-ceilinged factory, where partially uniformed workers in overalls or dark blue shirts moved about without any apparent order.

Farther on, at the back of the main yard, past a loading dock filled with six or seven semis, he found a row of small, two-story buildings painted a creamy white with dark blue trim.

"*Licenciado* Duelas, at your service."

"Belascoarán," said Héctor, shaking the lawyer's hand.

"We weren't expecting you…"

"I decided to accept your offer."

"The management's meeting right now. Come with me, and we can talk it over."

Héctor followed him through the inner offices, drawing curious glances from the secretaries he passed.

Which was the one who was eating a doughnut? he wondered.

They went through a polished wooden door into a conference room where four men sat in black leather chairs.

"*Señor* Guzmán Vera, company accountant"—a thin, affected man with a pair of wire-frame glasses perched on his nose. "*Señor* Haro"—young junior executive, fresh out of school with a degree in engineering. Héctor knew a hundred more like him. "*Señor* Rodríguez Cuesta, president and general manager"—silvery hair, dark complexion, bushy white mustache, tailored English suit. "Engineer Camposanto"—a stupid smile plastered onto a round face, too closely shaved for Héctor's liking, forty-ish.

"Welcome to Delex, *Señor* Shayne," began Rodríguez Cuesta. The other three men nodded their heads, as if the manager's greeting suddenly made him worthy of their esteem.

"Belascoarán Shayne," corrected Héctor.

Rodríguez Cuesta nodded.

Beyond the seated figures in the conference room, Héctor conjured up the image of the factory yard, the ovens inside the plant, the din of heavy machinery, the sweating workers.

He sat down without waiting to be asked, and Duelas took a seat by his side.

"The problem is a simple one," began the attorney. He seemed to be the designated spokesperson.

"The situation in the whole Santa Clara area right now is very delicate, and here at Delex, in particular, we are experiencing some very serious labor problems. As you know, this has not been a good year for business in general. And now with two men murdered in the last two months…The police have not been much help to us so far. Frankly, their work does not inspire confidence. What it boils down to is, we want the murders solved and the persons responsible brought to justice."

"Let me add," said Rodríguez Cuesta, "and I believe this information was not included in the report we sent you...but you should know that we have an interest in both of the firms involved, and that both companies have had problems with this same independent union."

"If you're looking to have the union take the fall for the murders, I don't see why you came to me. The cops ought to be more than willing to set that one up for you."

"That's probably what we'll end up doing...But in the meantime, we want to know who's really responsible, and what their motive was," answered the general manager.

What's it all about? What do they want? Héctor wondered.

"You can arrange for payment of your fee with *Señor* Guzmán Vera."

The accountant nodded.

"May I ask why you chose me for the job?"

"We know that you're an experienced engineer, with a master's from a university in the United States...It doesn't matter to us why you abandoned your career...We'd simply like to think that...how should I say it...that you're a member of the family. You already have a good understanding of how an industrial facility operates, you know what the problems are, and, in general, you're more likely to understand the way we think."

Loyalty among thieves, thought Héctor.

"Okay, it's a deal," he said, and regretted it as soon as the words were out of his mouth. What kind of mess was he getting himself into?

The five others smiled blandly, waiting for Héctor to leave.

Finally he stood up and left the room without saying another word. Guzmán the accountant followed him.

He kicked himself for having accepted. What the hell did he think he was doing? He remembered seeing two packs of fancy cigarettes on the table in the conference room: Philip Morris and

Benson and Hedges. There were no proletarian pretenses there. Couldn't he ever escape, forget his past? Was he condemned to live forever on the same side of the fence? Marked forever with that same Masonic-style stamp that he had unknowingly acquired on the very first day he entered the school of engineering, branding him as a foreman-accomplice to The Bossman for the rest of his life? Would it never be erased?

He was about to curse the day he decided to attend his first class instead of going to check out the girls in the School of Architecture cafeteria. But Guzmán Vera wisely took the initiative, and, with a superficial smile etched across his face, guided Héctor through the labyrinth of hallways to a tiny office, where he unlocked the door, took a seat behind his desk, and motioned Héctor toward an empty chair.

Héctor took special care to let the ash from his cigarette fall onto the carpet.

"How about a thousand pesos per day for the first fifteen days, plus expenses?"

"I don't think I'm going to charge you," Héctor told him. "Let me think about it for a minute."

The accountant stared at him in surprise.

"All right, I thought about it, of course I'm going to charge you. It'll be fifteen hundred a day for ten days, no expenses, I travel by bus. If after ten days I don't know who did it, I'll drop the case."

He got up.

"You can pay me at the end, don't worry about it."

Héctor closed the door behind him, and made his way back through the maze.

"What time do they break for lunch in the factory?" he asked the guard at the gate.

"One-thirty, boss. A bunch of them eat at that *lonchería* over there, or out here on the sidewalk, or at those stands down the block."

"Isn't there a workers' cafeteria inside the plant?"

"Sure there is, it's just that these days, nobody uses it anymore."

"Why is that?"

"Ever since they first threatened to go on strike, they've been coming here to eat. This is where they used to come for their meetings, anyway…"

Héctor walked slowly over from the Delex gate and sat wearily at one of the tables covered with a torn plastic tablecloth. He drank a red soda pop, one of those strange, brightly colored soft drinks he had come to love so much, both for their sweetness and because they were so uniquely Mexican.

"I heard that the workers stopped eating over at Delex so they could talk more freely during their lunch break…" he said to the woman at the *lonchería*.

"You heard from who…?" asked the woman, chasing after a little girl to wipe the snot from her nose. When she finished with the girl, she faced Héctor, put her hands on her hips, and asked him directly:

"Are you working for the company?"

"Well, yes, *Señora*…But I'm not a company spy, it's about something else. I was hoping I could talk to the boys from the union."

"That should be easy enough. You can find them at their lunch break." Turning away, the woman busied herself in the kitchen.

Héctor settled into his chair and scribbled some notes onto a worn pad:

Why do they call Zenón a dog?

The Sandinistas traveled through Costa Rica. Maybe some document issued there in 1932 would give me some clue about *don* Emiliano.

Why was there a whole case of soda pop in the back of the station wagon?

What does Rodríguez Cuesta really want from me? What are they afraid of besides the union?

He paused and considered.

In Mexico, competing companies weren't generally in the habit of bumping off each other's executives. Or if they were, Héctor hadn't heard about it. The ruling class had become too civilized for that.

The state had taken responsibility for that sort of violence instead. The state, or the corrupt pro-government unions.

He'd come away from his brief meeting with the Delex management with the distinct impression there was something they were afraid of. For one thing, they were far too willing to talk about their problems with the independent union. If that was all it was, the police would be more than happy to wrap the two murders and the union up together into one neat Christmas present for Rodríguez and his associates.

Héctor prided himself on his ability to look frankly into his own past, and, though it had not been easy to make the sudden break with job, wife, the only life he had ever known, he had gone ahead and started his new career as a private detective in a country where such a thing was unheard of, though anything was considered possible. As time passed, he managed to rationalize the new path he had taken, and the initially intuitive rejection of his earlier life as an engineer and efficiency expert with a nice house and a salary of 22,000 pesos a month. But for all its newfound rationality, his conviction was no less impassioned.

He knew that a big and powerful corporation didn't often have much to fear, beyond a confrontation with the government, or a massive wave of competition. And violence was normally connected only with the first alternative, not the second one. On the other hand, in recent years management had confronted the phenomenon of independent unionism from a thoroughly feudal perspective.

He couldn't say exactly why, but he had a sneaking feeling that the key to the mystery lay somewhere else altogether.

With two and a half empty hours ahead of him, he decided on a change of plans.

"Excuse me, *Señora*, when's the shift end?"

"The shift…three-thirty, young man."

He left four pesos on the table and went out, but not without first smiling warmly at the little girl crawling around nearby. To his surprise, and maybe only because no one had told her that he was still a stranger, she smiled back at him.

"Hi there, neighbor, what's happening?" asked the upholsterer as Héctor threw his coat at the coatrack.

"Just passing through."

With a red pen in hand, the upholsterer, perpetual hunter of odd jobs and seeker after sub-employment, continued his careful scanning of the want ads.

"Find anything?" asked Héctor, dropping into his armchair.

"Na…the guy next door with the stationery store wants me to do a job on an armchair for him, but the cheap son of a bitch says he won't pay any more than materials plus a hundred pesos."

Carlos Vargas, the upholsterer who sublet the plumber's half of the office in the mornings, was always in a good mood; and it seemed as though he was always looking for work. If they'd asked Héctor for a description he would have said: short, bearded, cheerful, spends all his time reading the want ads.

"There's a message from your brother on your desk."

Downtown, the sun was shining; the rain had stayed behind in Santa Clara.

"I'll be at the Havana Cafe until 12:30," said the note.

Héctor slipped back into his trench coat and headed for the door.

"You look tired, *maestro*," remarked the upholsterer.

"Yeah, I guess I am…Good luck finding some work."

When he opened the door he came face-to-face with Gilberto the plumber, his office mate since the good old days.

"Watch where you're going, pal," said the plumber.

"The super says you owe her for the cleaning," answered Héctor, unperturbed.

"I owe her for wiping my ass," countered Gilberto, more imperturbable still, dropping a heavy brown bag full of old pieces of pipe onto a desktop.

"Whatever you say, old buddy, just pay her and don't be an ass," said Héctor.

"Have her wash your balls next time and see if she charges you for that, too," said Carlos Vargas.

"Forget it, it'd take her an hour to dry 'em off. Yours, on the other hand…" but Héctor was out the door and crossing quickly toward the elevator before he got sucked into the verbal melee.

He walked along Artículo 123 in the direction of Bucareli. Boys were hawking papers on the street. There was a soccer game in front of the strange church that fronted the avenue, and a fistfight another twenty yards farther on. His eyes watered from the combined effects of fatigue and smog as he strolled along with his coat under one arm, thinking about his office. He wouldn't change it for the world. His frequent contact with the two master craftsmen and the strange nocturnal sewer expert kept him in touch with the real Mexico. Héctor himself completed the foursome; he was a craftsman as well, only with less skill and experience in his chosen profession. He was just another *mexicano* trying to make it in the Mexican jungle. It was up to him to defend himself against the myth of the super-detective, with its cosmopolitan and exotic delusions, to keep it from eating him alive. The puns, the dirty jokes, the gutter humor, gave him a daily dose of *mexicanidad*, Mexican-ness, which was reaffirmed again and again by the recurrent discussions of the rise in the price of soda pop and cigarettes, and the general and notorious cheapskatedness of hardware store owners, especially those of Basque-Spanish origin, and the post-weekend reports on the circus, or the latest TV comedian. And from a purely practical perspective, Héctor had three very efficient secretaries who took or conveyed messages without complaint, and kept his files. In return, Héctor was obliged to take job orders for the upholsterer and the plumber, quote prices on the repair of

Naugahyde love seats or broken faucets, and every now and then, take a message from the engineer's girlfriend.

If he were to go on listing positive factors he would have to include the fact that the office somehow fostered a remarkable climate of mental agility that sharpened his own ability to think. And that it offered a particular version of the city, with its view of the teeming and clamorous downtown streets, that Héctor was hopelessly in love with.

Arriving at Bucareli, he took a short detour to stop at a place that sold the best strawberry popsicles in the whole damn city.

His brother Carlos sat in front of an espresso and a Howard Fast novel.

"Qué pasa?" Héctor asked, tossing his coat onto a chair.

Héctor asked the waitress for a cup of coffee and some doughnuts, then waited for Carlos to open fire.

"Can you come over to my place tonight?"

"What time?"

"Nine or so."

"How about earlier."

"Eight all right?"

"Fine."

"It'll give the three of us a chance to talk about the famous inheritance."

"It's a weird feeling, isn't it?"

"Yeah, it sure is."

"Say, what do you know about the Delex Steel Company?"

"What are you doing mixed up with them?"

"You first."

"They've got three plants in Mexico City and two more in Guadalajara. The company's got a bad reputation even in the business world. People say it's full of crooks and shady deals. It throws a lot of financial weight, though. I don't know exactly who's behind it."

"You know anything about the union?"

"Which one, theirs or ours?" —→ *government and dependent*

"Yours."

"Well, a little…"

"Come on, Carlos, loosen up, I'm not a company spy."

"Yeah, I know…" He raised his hand to signal the waitress, and pointed to his empty cup.

"They're trying to break the union. They want to frame it for the murder of one of their engineers," Héctor said.

"We had an idea something like that was coming."

"Can you put me in contact with someone there?"

"Tomorrow."

"How about today?"

"I've never actually met any of the *compañeros* out there."

"Do you think you could come out with me?"

"What are you trying to do?" asked Carlos. Héctor sipped thoughtfully at his coffee before answering.

"I've just been hired by Delex to find the murderer."

"That doesn't sound too good. You know the union's about to go out on strike?"

"Yeah, I know."

"Well, I'll tell you what. I've got to take some proofs that I corrected yesterday back to the printer. And I could use some cash." Carlos smiled.

"Three-thirty, in the diner in front of the factory…Just five minutes, okay?"

"Okay. Isn't it going to get you in trouble if they see you hanging around with us?"

"Do I look like I care?"

"All right, I'll see you there. You can pay for the coffee," Carlos said, getting up from the table. "Ever hear anything from your girlfriend with the ponytail?"

Héctor shrugged. "I get a letter every now and then."

"Tough luck, old man," Carlos said, putting his hand on the back of Héctor's neck in a half-brotherly, half-fatherly gesture.

Héctor yawned. Surrounded by the noisy hubbub of the cafe, he sat thinking about how, in some inexplicable way, the roles had become reversed between him and his younger brother, and now Héctor was the baby of the family.

◇◇◇

When she saw him approaching, she left the shelter of the school doorway and came out to meet him. Her gray book bag hung from the same shoulder as the sling that held her arm.

Fascinated, Héctor took in the jumbled chatter of the white-bloused, plaid-skirted girls that fanned out across the street like a plague. The old man selling tamales recognized Héctor and smiled.

"Helluva fight, partner."

Héctor nodded.

"It's my guardian angel…" the girl greeted him. She curtsied slightly.

"Hello," said Héctor, for lack of anything else to say.

Together, they walked as far as Insurgentes. The sun threw bright sparks off the store windows. Three times it seemed as though Héctor was about to speak, but he only sucked more furiously on his cigarette. Somewhat uneasily, the girl watched him out of the corner of her eye.

"Aren't you coming?" she asked, with one foot up on the bus.

"Another time. Right now I've got too much to do."

Planted on the corner, he watched her walk to the back of the bus, take the last seat, and turn to look out the window behind her.

He didn't know what to say, or how to begin, and it occurred to him that what he liked to call his professional demeanor was no more than a reflection of the confused state of his own life. He wondered what some detective out of a mystery novel would have said.

He probably would have done the same thing Héctor had, saying nothing, silently protecting the girl. The difference was that he wouldn't have done it out of shyness.

Yawning, Héctor boarded another bus heading north.

Uneven lines of workers filed out of the plant gate. Several groups headed straight for the *lonchería*, and the tables filled up rapidly.

Héctor stood up.

"Which one's the guy from the ironworkers?" he asked a fat worker wearing a wool hat with a blue pom-pom, who motioned to a table at the front of the diner.

A hush fell over the room as all eyes turned to stare at Héctor. There was only the soft clink of soda-pop bottles on tabletops. He stepped forward decisively.

"I wanted to talk with someone from the union."

A tall man with a Zapata-like mustache motioned Héctor to a chair. Two other men sat at the same table: one balding, forty-ish, in blue coveralls, with sparkling eyes, and lips set in an eternal half smile around an eternally burning cigarette; the other a small bearded man with a cherry-red sweater and pants, and a pair of enormous, callused hands.

Héctor glanced toward the door, expecting to see his brother walk in at any moment. The flow of men from the factory hadn't stopped, and the *lonchería* got more crowded and quieter by the minute, in contrast to the noisy street outside.

"Delex has hired me to find out who killed the engineer Alvarez Cerruli…What they're probably going to try and do is frame you for the murder…Even though I'm working for them, I want to try and make sure that doesn't happen. The only way I can see to do that, is to find out who the real murderer is… And I need your help."

The three men looked at one another.

"Who the hell are you?"

"Héctor Belascoarán Shayne."

The name produced no reaction.

"Why don't you go ask Camposanto who did it?" shouted someone from one of the other tables.

The three men laughed.

"Why don't you go ask Camposanto to invite you to one of his parties?" asked the fat man with the wool cap at Héctor's back.

More laughter.

"Tell them we don't give a shit what they try and say we did," said the tall man. That was the end of the conversation.

Héctor got up from the table, walked over to where he'd been sitting before, laid a few pesos down beside an empty bottle of soda pop, and left.

The brightness of the sun outside made him blink. He felt sleepy. A group of young workers stood in front of the plant gate under the dark stare of a pair of security guards escorting a nonunion worker inside. They were selling copies of *The Vulture*, a small union paper. Héctor took a copy and tossed five pesos into the black-and-red can they held out in front of him.

"*Gracias, compa.*"

With the paper in hand, he passed by the gatekeeper, who greeted him with a glance of obsequious recognition mixed with annoyance.

Was the air inside the plant charged with tension? Or was lack of sleep starting to have its effect?

After phoning for permission, one of the secretaries agreed to make up a list of the home addresses of all the nonunion employees. Héctor smoked a cigarette while she typed.

"Who was *Señor* Alvarez's secretary?" he asked.

She pointed to a desk ten yards down the hall, where a young woman of about twenty-five was trying to reach some folders stacked on top of a file cabinet. Héctor looked at the smooth legs showing under her emerald-green skirt.

"Need a hand?"

"Yes, please…Just those yellow folders there. Thanks a lot."

Héctor passed them down to her.

"Were you Alvarez Cerruli's secretary?"

She looked at him for the first time.

"Police?"

Héctor shook his head.

"They tell me he wasn't very popular."

"He was very impersonal. Very, how should I say…rigid."

"What was the name of the other engineer who died a couple of months ago, do you remember?"

"Engineer Osorio Barba, yes, of course. He worked here until about two years ago. Alvarez Cerruli knew him well."

"Were they friends?"

The woman dropped her gaze.

"They knew each other very well."

"How did your boss act when he found out that Osorio was dead?"

"He spent the whole day shut up in his office."

"One last question."

"Excuse me, please, I've got to bring these…"

"Just one question." Héctor held her by the arm. Her muscles tensed under the pressure of his hand.

"Did anyone seem to be particularly saddened by Alvarez's death?"

"I've got to go now, I'll be back in a minute," she said, and disengaged herself from Héctor's grasp.

Héctor walked back to the first desk and took the list of addresses from the secretary.

Carlos was waiting for him at the plant gate, chatting with the men selling the union paper. He flagged Héctor down.

"I went over to the diner, but the guys from the committee had already left. Sorry I was late, but I couldn't get a hold of the guy who could have put me in touch with the people here."

"I can't figure out what the hell's going on around here. Why don't you tell me what's happening with the union? Maybe that'll help."

They walked together down the dusty street, leaving the two union men selling newspapers at the factory gate. The only other people left in the street were a pair of workers tossing coins with a *jicama* seller down at the corner.

Héctor couldn't help feeling like an outsider, strangely alien to the whole environment. It was starting to get on his nerves.

The Foreign Service office was closed afternoons, so after catnapping on one of the return buses, and reading *The Vulture* on the other (COLLECTIVE BARGAINING RIGHTS OR STRIKE! MANAGEMENT CALLS ON SCABS. NIGHT-SHIFT WORKERS SHUT DOWN MACHINE SHOP. ELECTRICAL WORKERS PLEDGE SOLIDARITY), he rented himself a car at an agency on Balderas, then bought a newspaper, hoping to find a movie theater where he could kill some time until seven o'clock. If things kept on going as they had so far, Héctor had another sleepless night ahead of him. It sounded like a rotten idea. He was about to give up on the movie, seduced by the thought of a shower and a decent meal, when he spotted an ad for a new Gabriel Retes film called *Chinameca: The Death of Zapatismo.*

He checked the time and smiled. Now wouldn't that be something, to find old *don* Emiliano waiting for him outside the movie theater? Come to town to see how they told his life in pictures?

His smile grew broader as he thought about the strange triangle he was caught up in now.

As he dried himself off brusquely after his shower, Héctor realized there was something about the whole tangled mess he didn't like. The music on the radio faded in and out. He ought to have his neighbor the electrician take a look at it. Outside the wind was blowing the dust around, and the tree in front of his window shook its branches melodiously.

He didn't like the fact that so many different characters had entered the story in such a short time. It felt as if he'd seen a thousand and one new faces in barely two days. He had a strange vision of a gigantic carousel filled with countless unknown faces, spinning endlessly around and around.

On the one hand were the boys with the Rambler wagon, on the other, the engineers from Delex, the men from the union. There were the faces of all the Sandinistas who may have fought alongside Zapata. There was Elena Ferrer's father, Alvarez Cerruli's ex-wife, and his maid still living in his house in Navarte, and Zenón, the "fag dog" foreman. But above all else, was the face of his mother; it wouldn't go away, appearing with every lurch of the bus, or in the pages of his book. And then there were the letters from the woman with the ponytail.

A parade of names: Duelas, Camposanto, Guzmán Vera, Osorio Barba…Other names insinuated themselves out of the mythical haze around Emiliano Zapata: Farabundo Martí, Porfirio Sánchez, Girón Ruano…Or in the girl's diary…

And somewhere in all of that, a secretary's legs under her emerald-green skirt, a woman in Italy in somebody else's bed, Elena's soft smile, her arm in a cast, Marisa Ferrer's see-through blouse.

All of that, plus the fatigue. It was enough to bring the whole thing crashing down on top of him.

But first, family, and then dinner. Putting on a white shirt, he hunted around in his closet for a necktie until he found one stashed away in a box of socks. It was gray knit, the child of another time. He put it on and started to tie the knot, then changed his mind. The time for compromise was over. He stripped the tie off and tossed it in the trash.

He left the house without turning off the radio.

Carlos was explaining to Elisa how the Echeverría government had tried to rebuild the economic base of the middle class after 1968. Héctor took a seat on the floor of the tiny roof-top apartment, poured himself a cup of coffee, and listened to the conversation. His sister leaned over and gave him a kiss.

"…For instance, just take a look at what happened to your classmates. Or yours," he said, motioning to Héctor. "Fifty percent of them ended up with high-paying jobs in some obscure government ministry created just for them, filling the ranks of bizarre, pointless institutions where there's never any work to do, and whose only purpose is to provide these people with jobs. For them, Echeverría reinvented the wheel. Instead of rebuilding the economic infrastructure, he simply ended up adding fat to the bureaucracy. Now, I'm not saying that some of these people didn't go into it with good intentions…but their good intentions didn't last for long. They got swallowed up into a new technocratic elite. And that's where they are today, feeding worms at the National Nopal Cactus Conservation Center…Slaving away at the Center for Resource Recovery…The Center for Partial and Inexact Studies, or The Sweet Potato Harvest Data Center…"

And he continued with a litany of names of real and made up institutions, which sounded to Héctor like the magical recitation of the holy rosary.

"…The Mongoloid Training Center…The National Center for the Study of Flatulence…The Center for the Development of the Grasshopper Harvest…The Natural Resources Institute… The Center for Retarded Studies…The National Banana Trust… A buddy of mine is writing his thesis on it. He's put together a list of sixty-three different institutions. Add that to the eighty-six or so I made up and you've got enough for a whole directory…"

"In Canada sometimes, when I was bored to death I'd make up names of imaginary saints," Elisa said, "like Saint Calvin Klein, Saint Van Camp, Saint Yves Saint-Laurent, there's a good one, or how about Saint Garbanzo of the Jolly Green Giant."

They all laughed.

"I've got a big can of tuna fish. Is anybody hungry?" asked Carlos.

"Sorry," said Héctor, "I can't stay long, I've got a dinner to go to."

"How are you doing?" Elisa asked him.

"Mixed up in other people's problems, as usual."

"Need any help?"

Héctor shook his head.

"So, what are we going to do about this?" She meant the inheritance.

"This whole thing's really upsetting to me, you know. But I'm not sure why."

"Hey, I hear you. It's got me all turned around, too. It's a weird thing. I suppose Héctor feels the same way."

"Well, one way or another, we've still got to deal with it."

"All right then."

Elisa took a pair of envelopes from her bag, while Héctor got up and went into the kitchen to look for an ashtray. He found one buried under some dirty dishes and rinsed it off.

"Go ahead," he said, "I can hear you."

"This one's a letter from Mama. Do you want to read it your-selves, or does someone want to read it out loud?"

"You read it," said Carlos.

"Fine with me," said Héctor from the kitchen.

My dearest children:

I know that by the time you read this letter I will no longer be alive. I hate the literary forms for this kind of thing, that's why I'm not going to write: 'I will have passed on,' or some such nonsense. I will be dead, and I hope that mine is an easy death, without complications. Unfortunately, my life was otherwise. You only know parts of the story. But I don't want to burden you with memories now. Each of you has your own. But now I'm getting off the subject…The story is a simple one: over the years and in the course of my life, I've acquired a modest amount of wealth.

By now, you will have already decided whether to distribute my estate yourselves, or to accede to the distribution as set out in the will. I'm not going to worry about it, since I know that none of you are too much in love with money. Now it's my responsibility to see that your father's wishes are also carried out. He asked me to give you a letter, and with it, the key to a safe-deposit box. I'm including these for you here. That's how he wanted it. So be it.

I wish you each the very best always. Think of me.

Shirley Shayne de Belascoarán.

"Wow," muttered Carlos.

They fell silent. In the apartment below them someone turned a TV on at full volume.

"It makes me feel like crying. I guess it doesn't hurt to admi it…" Elisa said after several minutes. "Now what?"

"Open the letter from Papa."

"It's just a short note, and a key. It says:

> 'The more complicated, the better. The more impossible, the more beautiful.'

> Box # 1627, Bank of the Americas, Central Branch. With this letter I authorize any one of my three children to open and use the contents of the aforementioned safe-deposit box.

> José María Belascoarán Aguirre.

"What's the old man got waiting for us?" wondered Carlos.

"How much do you remember him?"

Héctor emerged from the kitchen, checking his watch.

"The only thing I can think of for the money is that you should keep it," he said to Elisa. "You need it more than either of us."

"I don't want it," she answered firmly, shaking a stray lock of hair from her face.

"I've got to go now. What are we going to do?" asked Héctor.

"When can we get together and talk about this without you running off after five minutes?"

"How about tomorrow morning, at my office?"

"Twelve o'clock," suggested Elisa.

"Fine with me."

Héctor kissed Elisa on the cheek, patted Carlos on the back, and went out into the cold.

After driving around in circles for a while in the well-to-do neighborhood, he finally found the street and then the house. Two stories, set off by itself, with a small garden in front. The upper story was lit up as if there'd never been a rate increase. He rang the bell, thinking that the first thing he'd do when he got inside was turn off the lights in the den where no one was watching TV. Then he'd go around shutting off the rest of the lights, in the bathroom, the breakfast nook, the two bedrooms.

The past three months of celibacy somehow connected in Héctor's unconscious mind with the pictures from Marisa Ferrer's scrapbook and the idea of turning out the lights. He saw himself switching off the light on the bedside table, and then rolling over in the bed to cuddle up against his client's naked body. He rang the bell again, thinking that it was all the same to him whether the lights were on or off when he made love. Actually, he preferred to have the lights on. Elena opened the door, smiling timidly, and the detective blushed.

"It's my guardian angel…"

"I hope I didn't miss dinner."

"So it's you…you're the special guest…" she said, showing him into the house.

"Awful" was the only word Héctor could think of to describe the place, and he completely forgot his fantasy about turning out the lights. It was full of porcelain deer and lamps that didn't give off any light, ashtrays that never held any ash, and pictures that didn't tell a story. It was all very familiar to him; he even recognized the smell, like the smell of another house he'd been in once. That house had belonged to an engineer pulling down 22,000 pesos a month, married to a woman whose foremost thought was to get a new carpet for the dining room. He even remembered that he had once lived in that other house. But he managed to see that other Héctor as someone else he'd known once, a long time ago.

"You're very punctual, *Señor* Shayne."

"Belascoarán Shayne. The name's Belascoarán."

"You'll have to forgive Mama, she hasn't had time to study her script," said the daughter with a smile.

"What do you do when you've got a daughter who's too smart for her own good? In my parents' day, you sent her to a good Catholic school. It seems that in this case, it hasn't worked."

Marisa Ferrer was dressed in a resplendent black evening gown. The phrase "fits like a glove" came to Héctor's mind. As she moved, Héctor thought he could hear the melody of a far off rumba, like a movie sound track. Héctor imagined himself with a butter knife, slowly spreading the black material over the woman's skin. And she, either guessing his thoughts, intuiting them, or perhaps out of a sense of professional gallantry, paused silently for the detective to look her over. Then she took him by the arm and led him into the living room, which was separated by a folding screen from the dining room where three place settings were laid out on the table. A giant portrait of his hostess hung over the sofa. She was naked, lying sensuously across a polar-bear skin. Beside it were two pictures of a girl at five and then ten years old, and a painted seascape.

"Isn't it horrible?" asked Elena.

"Your mother's got remarkable taste."

"Mama, I told you to take it down from there."

"Darling, I'm sure *Señor* Belascoarán will have noticed," she pronounced his name slowly, smoothly, pausing after every syllable, "that I wasn't born to be an interior decorator."

She offered Héctor a cigarette from a music-box case that chimed out three notes from a polonaise. He took out his own pack of Delicados, and then lit his hostess's cigarette.

"I want to thank you for what you did for my daughter this morning. They called me from the school, and even though Elena won't say anything about it, I realized it must have been you who came to her rescue."

Héctor nodded, thankful for the girl's silence. He hadn't been born to save cats caught on rooftops. He played cleanly, expecting the same in return. Of course, he was more interested in the girl than in her mother. Putting aside *Señora* Ferrer's undeniable charm. Why should she be interested in him, after all? Did she just flirt automatically, as if by instinct, with whatever man she found in front of her? It was obvious she could have almost any man she wanted.

"It's time to eat," she said.

Héctor set his coat down, and Elena took it and hung it on a hook on the wall.

"You don't look like a detective anymore," she told him. "I hate to say it, but now you look like an architect's assistant who spends all day sitting at a drafting table."

As soon as they took their seats, a maid in a white apron appeared to serve the dinner.

"Elena, I hired *Señor* Belascoarán to help us out. Since you won't tell me anything, and since I know that you're in some kind of trouble…"

The girl interrupted the journey of spoon from plate to mouth. She stood up, and the napkin slid off her lap onto the floor.

"I liked you better as my guardian angel than as my mother's flunky," she said, and turning, walked slowly out of the room.

Héctor stood up.

"I'll be right back," he told the mother.

"So much for our peaceful little dinner," she said, smiling.

Héctor followed the girl's shadow down the hall, past a pair of bathrooms to the door of her room.

There were books along the walls, a sky-blue comforter, orange cushions on the floor, dolls from several years ago, still looking like new, a soft shag rug.

She kicked her shoes off and jumped onto the bed, snuggling up at the head of the bed near the pillows, and curling her legs up underneath her. Héctor stood in the doorway and lit a cigarette. He thought about it for a moment, then sat down on the floor, leaning his back against the wall.

"Got an ashtray?"

The girl tossed him a brass ashtray from her bedside table.

"Let's be on the level, Elena. I'm not going to work for you if you don't want me to. I'm happy to just walk away if you don't want me around to lend a hand. It's you that's got the problems, not me. Those boys this morning were serious, whatever it was they wanted. It's up to you. You decide, it's that simple."

The girl watched him in silence.

Héctor hesitated. Then he decided it was best not to risk alienating the girl by hiding something from her. A clean hand was the best.

"I read a scrapbook of your mother's, a few newspaper clippings about your accident, and several pages out of your diary."

"My diary?"

"A few pages. Photocopies."

"What an idiot I am."

"I tell myself that every day. For all the good it does me. Is it a deal, or isn't it?"

"I don't even know anything about you. I don't even know who you are."

"It's a long story, Elena. It's a very long story and I don't know that if I told it to you you'd understand, because I don't even understand it very well myself. I wouldn't know where to start."

"If you want to know my story, you'll have to tell me yours, too."

"The problem is I don't keep a diary."

"I'll bet you laughed when you read it."

"I don't laugh very often."

"Let me think for a minute…You seem honest enough, and you seem like you really want to help…Shit. I guess I could use some help, after all."

"They teach you to talk like that in Catholic school?"

"Where did you go to school?"

"It's been over ten years now since I finished high school."

"The public school kids aren't half as tough as we are."

"Tomorrow, after school?"

The girl nodded, and Héctor left the room.

Her mother was waiting for him in the living room. She had company.

"*Señor* Belascoarán, I'd like you to meet *Señor* Burgos, an old friend of the family."

Héctor shook the man's hand, it was sweaty, and squeezed his tightly. Behind the hand was a dark man, about forty years old, curly black hair, wearing a leather jacket, and a silk scarf around his neck.

Burgos, thought Héctor. Another name on the list. He had cold, teary eyes. Snake's eyes. All right, enough already, it was starting to sound like a Graham Greene novel.

He's an ugly motherfucker. So what?

"What's the verdict?"

"Same as before. I'll let you know how it's going."

Marisa Ferrer accompanied Héctor to the door, after a brief "Just a minute, Eduardo."

Once at the door, she put her hand in Héctor's, but he quickly pulled away and lit a cigarette.

"Just one thing, *Señora*, I don't want anybody to know that I'm working for you. No one." He gestured toward the other room.

"Nobody knows, don't worry. Did she tell you anything?"

Héctor shook his head.

"I want to thank you again for what you did today. Not just because you saved Elena from those thugs. She suddenly seems to feel safer now, more confident. She spent all afternoon joking about how much fun it was to have a guardian angel."

"Guardian angel my ass," muttered Héctor when he was back out in the street, with the cold air against his face. A frigid wind blew down from the mountains. "Who's going to look after me?"

The rented VW had a radio with rear-mounted stereo speakers, and a light on the rearview mirror. Héctor turned them both on and ran through the list of Delex employees while he listened to some rhythmic, melancholy blues.

Camposanto—680 Insurgentes South, Apartment L.

He headed down Insurgentes toward Napoles, with the windows open, so as to get the most out of the cold mountain air.

> *The night is a man's best friend. A woman's, too. Believe it, because it's true. Is your heart beating faster than normal? Do you feel* strange? *Don't worry. El Cuervo is here to keep you company.*

He was startled by the voice on the radio. A little bell started ringing in his head.

> *Atahualpa Yupanqui sang it best when he said: God made the night for man to conquer.*

*Ain't it the truth? Don't despair. Don't feel lonely. We may be alone, but we still have each other. Solidarity out of the solitude, that's our motto. This is El Cuervo, coming to you on radio Station XEFS, Mexico City. Right now I want to send out a big hello to the workers at the Vidriera Mexico glassworks. Vidriera Mexico has been holding back overtime pay, and we all know that's not right. Everybody deserves a fair wage for their labor.*

*Animo, my friends, good luck in your struggle. I'm going to dedicate this next song to you, it's a song of struggle from the campesinos of Peru. The group Tupac Amaru, with "Tierra Libre."*

The music filled the car. Héctor stopped at a red light, and a distant face surfaced out of his memory: Valdivia, skinny little Valdivia. With that voice it had to be him. It was the same voice he remembered from grade school, winning recital contests: "Ten cannons on a side, a strong stern wind, full sail flying…"

The little car responded to the accelerator, and leapt forward down Insurgentes.

It must have been around ten o'clock. He checked his watch, stifling a yawn: 10:25.

Probably too late to catch Camposanto at home.

*You're tuned to XEFS, Mexico City, and the El Cuervo Show. The master of the night. From now until the exact moment when the sun rears its bald head over the horizon and spoils everything. The only program that ends when Count Dracula closes the lid on his coffin. Free from the absurd limits of the clock, and tied to the even more absurd limits imposed on us by the rotation of the earth…I've got a guy on line one who says he's going to run away from home and wants to talk about it with us first. Lines two and three are open, just call fifty-one twelve two forty-seven, or fifty-one thirteen one-nineteen. Your direct connection to El Cuervo.*

Héctor pulled up in front of 680 Insurgentes, and divided the next ten minutes between yawns, vague speculation as to the location of Apartment L, the story of the kid who wanted to run away from home, and a feeling of desperation caused by his own lack of foresight, the result being that he had only six cigarettes left to last him the rest of the night. The building had a large garage, with a heavy mesh door across it. There were four cars parked inside, two Ramblers, a Datsun, and a Renault station wagon. Which one would it be? He tried to remember if he'd seen one of them that morning in the factory parking lot.

> *And now, some more music to please your soul during these dark hours when the life force is strongest.*
>
> *Of course, I'm assuming that you're all awake because you want to be. If that's not the case, if you're slaving away the night at some dead-end job, just remember, the night time is the right time. It's the best time to be alive. Transfer to the swing shift, and sleep in the morning.*

Not a bad idea, thought Héctor. Shit, El Cuervo, who would have guessed it.

> *The night is a time of solitude, it's the time when the mind works most clearly, when the ego diminishes, and melancholy reigns. A time when we feel the urgent need for a helping hand, a friendly voice, when we feel most able to do our share and lend a hand where help is needed.*
>
> *You're listening to the El Cuervo Show, with your friend and host, El Cuervo Valdivia, your bridge to the cosmos, a link between brothers from the depths of the darkness.*
>
> *I have here a card from a young woman named Delia. Delia says she wants to fall in love again.*
>
> *It seems that things haven't gone too well for her in the past. She says she's been divorced twice and now she's eating her heart out with loneliness. Is there anyone out there who wants to lend a hand?*

After ten minutes there were six volunteers who were willing to help Delia give it another try.

Delia was followed by a poem by Cesar Vallejo, songs from the Spanish Civil War, a set of songs by Leonard Cohen, a call for blood donors, type AB negative, and a request for food for some strikers in the Escandon neighborhood, which was answered by the offer of three breakfasts at the Guadarrama Cafe and a pot of hot chocolate prepared by some people in the neighborhood. Next came several cryptic personal messages: "Lauro, don't forget to buy it," "Anastasia is waiting for her friends on her birthday," "For anyone in the experimental physics class at CCH, call Gustavo at such and such a number, there's an exam tomorrow and he can't find his notes," et cetera.

A middle-aged couple drove away in the red Rambler. A young man drove two elderly men away in the Datsun and then returned alone.

At twelve-thirty, with El Cuervo coming on stronger than ever, and as Héctor was counting his last three cigarettes, engineer Camposanto emerged from the house, dressed in a finely tailored gray suit and a red tie. Héctor followed him.

*A helping hand on the airwaves. The El Cuervo Show. A friendly voice to help all of you caught in the clutches of cold, insomnia, fear, and despair. And especially for all you wage slaves out there.*

*Your compañero of the airwaves.*

*The city sleeps. Or so they say. But you and I know different. Suppose it was true, then let her sleep, the ungrateful bitch. We are the sentinels of darkness, watching over the nightmare sleep of this old whore who calls herself Mexico City. While she sleeps, we live, ever ready to offer a cloak of solidarity in the middle of the darkness.*

*Now listen to me, this is a message to the two traffic cops at the corner of Michoacan and Nuevo Leon: put the traffic light back to automatic already. People aren't going to keep dishing out your little bribes forever. For more information, you can talk to the officers themselves.*

> *They're parked in car number 126 in front of a diner at the intersection.*

Camposanto left his vehicle parked at the corner of Niza and Hamburgo. Héctor hated having to leave El Cuervo behind. His intuition told him that he was going to spend another sleepless night for nothing, that the engineer was going to go have a couple of drinks alone in a bar, and that no one would approach him, no one would speak to him. Another wasted night.

And that's how it turned out.

> *If you're the kind of person who thinks the night is a reign of terror, if you wake up in a cold sweat, if it scares you when you hear the siren of an ambulance, if your children have nightmares, if this is the worst moment of your life, if you've got to make some terrible decision… Don't forget. El Cuervo's waiting for your call…Brothers and sisters, the night is long…*

# Chapter Five

If you were to ask me why he's a private detective, I wouldn't be able to tell you. Obviously there are times when he would rather not be, just like I have moments in which I would rather be anything but a writer.

—Raymond Chandler

In February 1977, Isabelita Peron, resembling more than anything else a character from an old vampire movie, made it known through the press that she was willing to confine herself to the seclusion of a convent immediately upon her release by military authorities. The sinister Argentine dictator General Videla miraculously escaped unharmed from the third recent attempt to blow his ass to smithereens; and the Mexican plumber Gilberto Gómez Letras, taking advantage of the fact that his office mate had let his subscription to *Excelsior* expire, signed him up instead for the next six months of *Sporting World*. Holland was shaken by a general strike. There were one hundred seven suicides reported for the month in Los Angeles. Graft was exposed in the manufacture of traffic lights in Mexico City. Marisa Ferrer, actress and cabaret star, was invited to attend the Chihuahua Film Festival. The radio show with the best ratings was the El Cuervo Show on XEFS. And Héctor Belascoarán Shayne logged a total of fifty-one hours without reaching the state technically known as "deep sleep." Even so, at 6:45 in the morning, yawning, with heavy-lidded, bloodshot eyes, and an unidentified pain in his back, he watched from the *lonchería* as the workers entered the Delex plant across the street. Even at a distance he could tell that engineer Camposanto wasn't in such great shape himself, having stayed out drinking alone until 3:30 A.M. in a Zona Rosa dive called *El Elefante*. He saw the tall unionist from the day before, and his two companions, waving their arms dramatically as they talked, escorted in by a group of their fellow workers. He watched Rodríguez Cuesta drive up in his Cadillac, and thought again that the company president was hiding something behind that facade of self-assurance and power. What was he afraid of? Héctor left fifty pesos and his phone number with the woman at the *lonchería*, his new field headquarters, and asked her to phone him if something happened. He smiled at the little girl playing on the floor, and went out.

The walls had been hit again during the night, and now they were covered with bright red letters calling for a WORK STOP-PAGE AT 11.

Héctor couldn't help but see similarities in the festive arrival of the girls for morning classes at the Catholic school. Both events shared a party atmosphere flavored with defiance. From his post inside a candy store he watched Elena's arrival, thinking he ought to either follow her or accompany her all the way from home. Otherwise his absurd strategy of waiting for her at the school yard might turn out to be nothing more than an inoffensive hobby, while her enemies intercepted her somewhere on her way to school.

It depressed him to think how much he was a creature of habit, motivated more by rituals than the need for effective action. He spent the rest of the morning in the office of an old school friend who worked in the Foreign Service.

A 1500 peso *mordida* gave him access to an old coffer that served as the last resting place for the dust-covered files of the Mexican Embassy in Costa Rica in the nineteen thirties. In the end, when it felt as if he'd never be able to wash the fine dust off his fingertips, he came away with three names and three faded photographs.

Isaías Valdez. Mexico City.
Eladio Huerta Pérez. La Tolvanera, Oaxaca.
Valentín Trejo. Monterrey, Nuevo Leon.

Their ages corresponded, the dim pictures offered the suggestion of a likeness. He wrote down their Mexican addresses, and went out into the hall where he bought a soda pop from a machine to cool his parched throat.

Then he headed back to his office, falling asleep a couple of times on the Metro, standing up, like a horse.

The upholsterer was reading the want ads in *Excelsior*. The plumber hadn't arrived yet.

"Anything for me?"

"Na. Just a couple of letters. You owe me the tip for the mailman."

"You know what, *Señora* Concha called you the other day, I forgot to tell you about it. She wanted you to come by and pick up some..."

"Some slipcovers...Dammit, as little work as there is and you forget to give me the message."

Héctor stared at the floor in embarrassment.

He dropped into the armchair without bothering to take off his coat, loosen his belt, or remove his shoulder holster. He leaned back in the squeaky chair, his old leather-covered friend, kicked off his shoes, and stretched until his body felt as though it was going to fall apart. The distant rumble of traffic lulled him to sleep.

"*Órale pues*," called a voice out of the shadows.

"*Ándale*, Héctor," came a woman's voice from the other side of the blackness.

"I can't," Héctor confessed.

"Coffee?" suggested Carlos.

"I can't open my eyes. I really can't."

"We brought the stuff from Papa. Come on, *ándale*, Héctor, time to wake up."

Héctor finally managed to get his eyes open, and the vague shadows took shape in the light of the room. It all felt like part of a movie he'd seen several times before.

"What time is it?"

"Twelve-thirty," answered his sister.

"How long were you sleeping?" asked his brother, Carlos.

The two of them sat together on the edge of his desk, next to a cardboard shoe box.

"Only an hour."

Héctor tried to stand up.

"How long has it been since you got any real sleep?"

"Night before last I slept for a couple of hours."

"You look kind of green," observed Carlos.

"No, I'd say it's more gray. A gray-green," said Elisa.

"You don't know how happy it makes me feel to have a couple of comedians come and wake me up. Can you get me a soda pop…Over there behind the filing cabinet, in the wall."

Elisa jumped down lightly from the desk and went to find the secret compartment.

"What's this? The office safe?"

The sweet taste of Orange Crush brought Héctor back to life.

"What's going on?" asked Carlos. "You having a hard time with your work?"

"What do you keep it up for?" Elisa asked. "I can understand why you did it in the first place. But I can't for the life of me figure out why you don't move on and do something else now that your life has changed. You're free now. So why not find something better to do?"

"Why should I? It's a job like any other."

"Now that's a hell of a good reason." Carlos laughed.

"Hand me my shoes, willya?"

Carlos tossed the shoes at Héctor. He was still waiting for the mist to clear completely; it lingered somewhere in the back of his brain and now and then sent waves of fog rolling across his field of vision. Rubbing his face energetically with the palms of his hands, he stretched himself and then jumped up.

"*Aaahhhhgggguuujj.*"

"All right, now let's get started."

The phone rang.

"It's for you," said Carlos, and he passed him the receiver.

"*Señor* Shayne?" It was Marisa Ferrer. Héctor sensed the tension in her voice and for once he ignored the confusion caused by his double surname.

"Elena's been kidnapped. They just called me from the school…"

"I'm on my way."

He hung up and looked around for his coat.

"What's up?"

"A girl's been kidnapped. Do you guys mind putting this thing off for a while?"

"No problem," answered Carlos. "Just let me know when you've got some time."

The telephone rang again.

"No, the upholsterer's not here right now…What's that? A message? Sure, just a minute, let me find a pen…" Elisa put one in his hand. "Okay. Three meters of number one hundred seventeen BX, blue and black. *Señora* del Valle. Yes, of course. I'll give him the message."

"Can I give you a ride somewhere," offered Elisa when he got off the phone.

"Do you have a car?"

"No, just the gardener's motorcycle."

"How about driving my rent-a-car?"

"What kind is it?"

"It's a VW." Héctor buttoned his coat.

Elisa held out her hand for the keys.

"I guess I'll be going," said Carlos, picking up the shoe box. "I'll hold on to this for safe keeping."

"Sorry about this, brother."

"Don't worry about it."

As they were going out the door, the telephone rang again. Héctor hesitated, then went back.

"There were some shots and now they're fighting at the gate. I called like you asked me to…" It was the woman from the *lonchería*. She hung up. So that's how it was going to be…first nothing, and now everything all at once.

"What is it this time?"

"There were shots fired in the factory, or something like that."

"I'm going over there," said Carlos.

"Give me the box, then," said Elisa.

"I'll be out there as soon as I can."

"It's got nothing to do with you, Héctor. Stay out of it. It's between the union and the company…It's not your problem."

"I'll be out there all the same," Héctor insisted.

Carlos shrugged.

"I hope you know what you're doing."

"What factory?" Elisa asked, as Héctor took her by the hand and pulled her toward the elevator.

"Everything at once and I can barely keep my eyes open."

"What did I tell you?"

"What did you tell me about what?"

"About your job, it's crazy…"

"I wouldn't trade it for the world."

"I kind of guessed," said Elisa as the elevator doors slid shut.

The phone started to ring again in the office, but this time there was no one there to answer it.

He made his way through the ranks of nuns until he got to the head sister's office. He had dozed briefly, fitfully, in the backseat of the car, unable to get the picture of Elena, with her arm in a cast, out of his mind. And the image of the one girl brought him around again to the image of another woman thousands of miles away. Elisa pushed the pedal to the floor, but heavy midday traffic held them back.

Héctor remembered the upholsterer saying something about some mail for him…he felt in his coat pocket, there it was. Still, it would have to wait for a more opportune moment.

And the message for the upholsterer? He'd left it on the desk, scribbled in the margin of one of the old newspapers they used as stationary in their office. Héctor hoped he'd see it there.

"Who are you?" demanded the nun from behind a pair of glasses thick as Coke bottles. She was as stiff as her starched white habit.

"Detective Belascoarán Shayne, ma'am." Elisa, standing behind him, couldn't keep from smiling at the strange combination of the exotic profession and the familiar family name. She'd heard the name so many times, as a child in school, over and over again, almost always mispronounced. And now to think that her brother was a private detective... He's crazy, she thought. Crazy like everybody else.

"I'm working for *Señora* Ferrer," he explained, showing his license. The sister passed her hand over it like a blind woman reading Braille, with her eyes still on the detective.

"Where did it happen?"

"Out in the playground. She was in gym class."

Héctor raced out of the office and down the stairs, heedless of the shouts that followed him from the principal's office.

A couple of dozen girls in blue shorts and white shirts were scattered around the school yard, clustered into small groups, talking. The gym teacher, a thin, fibrous woman with the look of a retired British tennis pro, came over to talk with Héctor. Elisa followed a few yards behind him, cradling the shoe box in her arms.

"They came in over there," the woman told him without waiting to be asked. "Elena wasn't in the class, because of her arm, you understand? She was lying down on that table over there, in the sun."

She pointed to a broken-down old desk. Héctor looked at it as if it were important.

"There were two of them, with guns...They were both so young. Both of them had black hair, and one of them was wearing dark sunglasses."

"The other one was wearing a green sweatshirt," volunteered a girl in the circle that had begun to form around them.

"They went straight for her and grabbed her and took her away. They pointed their guns right at me."

"Me, too."

"They were pointing at everybody."

"The one in the sweatshirt grabbed her by the neck and made her walk really fast."

"Did they say anything? Did Elena say anything?"

"She shouted when they pushed her. She said that her arm hurt."

"What did she say exactly?"

"Leave me alone, you're hurting me, something like that."

"Did she seem very surprised?"

"Yes, very," one girl told him.

"No, not very," said another.

Héctor left them discussing the kidnapping among themselves and ran through the gate and out onto the street, glancing rapidly up and down the block. Across the street, the old tamale seller stood staring at him. Héctor crossed over, with Elisa following close behind.

"You saw them," Héctor said. It was a statement, not a question.

"I don't want any trouble, mister."

"Look, I'm not with the cops."

"I don't want any trouble, mister."

The conversation went on like that for about five minutes.

Finally, the old man handed him a small piece of paper.

"The bastards... They were driving that same Rambler station wagon. Here's the license number. But you didn't get it from me, okay?"

"I found it on the ground," Héctor said. He dropped the slip of paper and stooped to pick it up again from the sidewalk.

The old man smiled.

◇◇◇

"But what the hell's the point? Where's the challenge, what makes it all worthwhile?" he asked himself as he stretched out in the backseat of the northbound VW, his sister at the wheel. He dozed off as they drove along Ferrocarril Hidalgo past Villa de Guadalupe, but the question followed him into his dreams.

What bothered him wasn't the peculiar, violent rhythm of the last few days, or the uncontrollable momentum that propelled him along, forcing him to choose, or better yet, forcing him to accept the choices that the course of events had already pushed him into. The thing that bothered Belascoarán was the "why" of it all, why he had gone ahead and gotten himself into such a mess. Which part of his confused mind was it that had set him off on this fiery road to glory, along these three parallel paths? The basic question seemed simple enough, but all he had were three different answers that each accounted only for their own part of the complicated story: (a) There was something he liked instinctively about the teenage Elena Ferrer, with her arm in a cast; there was something that attracted him in the role of silent protector. (b) He thought that by wading into the muck surrounding the murder of the two engineers, he'd find a way to repay the debt he'd incurred during all those years he'd worked as an engineer himself. It wasn't that he owed anything to the profession. That wasn't it at all. Rather, it was a debt that came out of his willing submission to the status quo, his disdain for the workers, all the times he'd driven through the working-class neighborhoods like a man traveling through a disaster zone. He needed to go back to where he'd started from and prove to himself that he had changed. And, of course, tied up with the rest of it was the problem of keeping the independent union from being framed for the murders. (c) He wanted to look into the living eyes of the real Emiliano Zapata, he wanted to know if the country the old revolutionary had once dreamed of was still possible, to see if the old man could somehow communicate some of the spirit and conviction that had inspired his crusade. Although he didn't believe for a minute that Zapata was actually still alive, the simple act of delving into the past, searching for the clues of his fugitive existence, seemed to bring the old man that much closer to life.

That's more or less how things settled out in the mind of Héctor Belascoarán Shayne, a detective by trade, thirty-one years old, with the good luck and the misfortune to be born and raised a Mexican. Divorced, without children, in love with a woman far away. The occupant of a grimy office on Artículo 123, and a minuscule apartment in the Roma Sur. With a master's degree in industrial engineering from an American university, a certificate in detection from a Mexican correspondence school; a fan of private-eye novels and a connoisseur of Chinese food, a mediocre driver, lover of parks and forests, owner of a .38 revolver; a little rigid, fairly shy, mildly sarcastic, excessively self-critical; who one day, on his way out of a movie theater, broke with his past, and started his life all over again, until he found himself where he was now: crossing over Puente Negro in the backseat of a VW bug, dressed in a wrinkled trench coat, and overcome with a sleepiness that poured from his mouth with every yawn.

"Go straight along here then take the third right."

"Yes, boss."

"What's going on with you these days?" he asked his sister.

Elisa smiled into the rearview mirror.

"Do you need a chauffeur or don't you?"

Héctor didn't answer.

"When I need an analyst I'll let you know."

"All right, all right. It's just that lately you seem kind of, well, you know…"

Héctor rubbed his sister's neck gently from behind. Without looking back, she tilted her head to squeeze his hand between her cheek and shoulder.

They could see the crowd gathered in front of the plant from two blocks away. A pair of patrol cars blocked the road.

Héctor got out of the car, showed his license, and they let them through.

"What's going on?"

"They wouldn't say. Drive over toward that *lonchería.*"

Some two hundred workers formed a compact mass behind the Delex gate. In front of the iron railing stood a squadron of armed policemen, and behind them, a few dozen scattered workers. Ten yards back from the gate there was another mass of workers brandishing sticks and pipes, with a bald man in a tan suit egging them on. Carlos stood near the gate, talking with the workers from *The Vulture.*

"*Qué pasa?*" Héctor asked him. "What's going on?"

"Nothing. That's a bunch of scabs over there," and he motioned with his chin toward the group of armed workers outside the gate, "who they tried to bring into the plant. But if we can hold out another hour until the guys from the swing shift get here, we'll have them beat."

"What happened before?"

"We were in the middle of the work stoppage," answered a short worker with a piece of gauze taped across his cheekbone, "and one of these damn scabs up and hits Gustavo with a pipe, so like an idiot I go over there to see what's the matter, and the son of a bitch nails me, too. Well, of course, the *compañeros* got pretty pissed when they saw what happened, and they went and chased this guy all over the factory, and when they came running out into the yard, the guards shot into the air to scare them off. Then the foreman showed up and he fired me. For aggression, he said, the lousy son of a bitch. But they had it all figured out beforehand, because when the guards pulled me out of the plant, they had these guys waiting here with that Uncle Tom from the pro-government union federation…They all come from around Santa Julia. I've seen one of them around before, they call him El Chicai, he lives over a pool hall behind the market…But anyway, they screwed up, because the boys all came out to the gate and here we are now…And then the cops showed up."

The crowd of workers behind the gate started to chant: "Dogs! Dogs!" and then broke into a chorus of *We Shall Not Be Moved*. The other workers scattered around the yard joined in. The security guards advanced on the gate and the gang of scabs pulled away.

A rumor of voices could be heard approaching in the distance.

"Who's that?" Héctor asked.

A column of marching men broke through the police roadblock.

"Union workers from a rolling mill around the corner. It's their lunch hour and they've come to lend a hand…Just wait and see if it doesn't come to this now…" The short man gestured roughly with his hands.

There were about 200 of them and they walked arm in arm in rows of seven or eight. Most of the scabs started to drift away, leaving only a nucleus around the man in the tan suit, and even they retreated another twenty yards so as not to be caught between the approaching column and the workers behind the plant gate.

The men inside the yard saw what was happening and increased the volume of their chanting. They surged past the three guards blocking the gate, scaled the steel grating and greeted the arriving workers with shouts and hugs.

"Whew," said Carlos, "that was close. The second shift'll be here in another twenty minutes and that'll be it for today. Now we have to find a way to get you men back inside."

"Here I go," said the short worker.

"Remember, they can't fire you for what happened in there. You were attacked and didn't retaliate. Go on in and return to your station," said a tall man behind them.

The short one ran toward the gate and climbed over, evading a pair of guards who tried to stop him. His fellow workers welcomed him back with cheers.

"I'm going," Héctor said.

"I told you it didn't have anything to do with you," answered Carlos.

"I was glad to be here."

"I wonder if the boss man saw you."

"I couldn't care less."

There was no one in the office. From the window he watched Elisa drive away on her motorcycle, and then went and picked up the telephone, hunting in the old newspapers on his desk for a name and a number. Sergeant García. He dialed the number of the traffic cop who sold him information at fifty pesos a shot and read him the license number from the green Rambler station wagon. After a few minutes García came back on the line.

"Stolen. Two weeks ago. Do you want the owner's address?"

"No thanks. Won't do me any good."

"I'll put it on your bill. That's three you owe me now."

"I'll be by the end of the month…In the bar?"

"That's the place." García hung up.

Next Héctor called a detective agency in Monterrey, asking them to track down the man who had obtained a passport in Costa Rica in 1934, listing his residence in that city. Then he phoned the police station in Ixtepec, but the recalcitrant bureaucrat who took the call refused to give out any information on La Tolvanera.

He remembered having passed through there once, crossing the Isthmus of Tehuantepec from Oaxaca on his way to Veracruz, but that was all.

He jotted the third name, with the corresponding Mexico City address, onto a scrap of paper, and wrote a note for Gilberto, asking him to check discreetly whether the man still lived there, without actually going to the house itself. He paper-clipped a fifty-peso bill onto the note and set it to one side of the desk.

After that he telephoned Marisa Ferrer, but the maid said only that she had gone out without leaving a message.

Then he turned his attention to the girl's diary. If there were clues, that's where they had to be. It was just a matter of finding them.

He got up and took a soda from the secret cupboard. He lit a cigarette, and remembered he was still hungry. He cursed his cold-bloodedness, his capacity for calm. He hated his inability to show emotion. So he spent five minutes wondering if Greenjacket and Armgrabber were capable of hurting the girl. For an instant, he felt a kind of rage, and then returned to his typical coolness. He took a last swig from the soda pop and confronted the diary.

A quarter of an hour later he summed up his notes:

1. Bustamante is a girl.

It took him a while to figure out that the old habit of calling friends by their last names that prevailed in his own school days now extended to Catholic girls' schools as well. He finally figured out that the strange situation of a boy named Bustamante with a *boyfriend* was really just a *girl* named Bustamante with a boyfriend.

2. The class notes mixed into the diary had nothing to do with the case.

All the same, it would be necessary to talk to Gisela, Bustamante, and Elena's other friends at school.

3. Elena has something worth over 50,000 pesos. Whatever it is, it's dangerous, and she can't get rid of it. And *who knows how she got it?*

That was the key to the whole thing right there. Es. and G. (Esteban? Eustolio? Esperanza?) wanted whatever it was she had.

4. But it all has to do with something she knows about her mother and her mother doesn't know she knows. Could she have taken the 50,000-peso-whatever-it-is from her?

No, because then there would be an allusion to the possibility of her mother's discovering that something was missing…In that case, Elena must have some kind of information about her mother. She knows something; it's not that she has something her mother owns. Whatever it is, she got it from someone other than her mother.

Where then to pull the first thread? From Marisa Ferrer, of course.

He picked up the telephone and dialed her number again. The maid gave him the same answer as before, and Héctor left his office number and asked that she phone him.

If I wasn't so damn tired, I'd go get something to eat, he told himself, ignoring the noises in his belly and dropping down into the old armchair. He glanced at the gallery of photos on the wall, a corpse, Emiliano Zapata, a girl with her arm in a cast, and fell asleep without even bothering to take off his shoes.

"He's gonna drive himself crazy."

"In my village there was this guy who used to just sleep any old place, and then one day he fell asleep out in front of this faggot's house, and when he woke up the guy was giving it to him in the rear."

"I think he sleeps here all the time so he doesn't have to make his bed at home. He's kind of a slob, our *don* Belascoarán."

Héctor slowly raised one eyelid, like someone opening the creaking blinds in a bank window. Gilberto the plumber and Carlos Vargas the upholsterer stood watching him with motherly attention.

"Watch out, the bat's waking up…"

"He's got vampire eyes…"

"Wha's happnin'?"

Each one held a sandwich. They grinned broadly at Héctor.

He jumped up suddenly and grabbed the food, one sandwich in each hand.

"Put it on my bill," he said, glancing around for his wrinkled coat.

"Hey, I've been robbed…"

"You've got a message there on the desk about a job, and I left you a note about some extra work I've got for you," he said, speaking first to the upholsterer and then the plumber.

"You can keep the sandwiches," said Gilberto. "Just don't forget next time it's your turn to buy the sodas."

"Did you pay the super for the cleaning yet?"

"Take, take, take, that's all I ever hear. And with inflation the way it is…"

"The only inflation you know about comes in your old lady's belly every year," interjected the upholsterer dryly.

The plumber winced.

"Watch out, buddy…you can dish it out, but we'll see if you can take it, too…"

"What time is it?" Héctor interrupted.

"Just after three."

Héctor couldn't wait for the elevator and flew down the stairs instead, bracing himself on the handrail at every landing to keep himself from falling head over heels.

Once in the street, he jumped into his car and jammed his foot onto the accelerator.

He hated the city and he loved it. He was getting used to living in the midst of contradictions.

He bought a pack of cigarettes at a stand in front of the Carousel Cinema, and carefully scrutinized everyone arriving for the showing of the movie about Zapata. A pair of old *campesinos* caught his eye, but they were only in their fifties. Too young, after all. No ninety-five-year-old men showed up to buy a ticket.

He got back in the car and headed out toward Pedregal.

One seventeen Aguas Street was a starchy-looking place, like a papier-mâché castle without damsels or dragons, painted a creamy gray and surrounded by a gray railing which blocked a clear view into the large garden. Several dogs barked at him and he wondered if they weren't the real masters in that upper-class city within a city, called Pedregal de San Angel.

"Who is it?" asked an electronically distorted voice through the intercom.

"I'm looking for the ex-wife of engineer Alvarez Cerruli."

"I'll see if she's available. Who's calling for her?"

"Belascoarán Shayne."

He pronounced his name twice and waited.

At last a gardener came to open the gate, and, protecting him from the dogs, guided Héctor to the door.

The woman received him in a modishly decorated sitting room. She carried her forty-odd years well, dressed like a North American housewife of thirty, in a tan skirt, a long-sleeved cream-colored blouse, and her hair tied back with a ribbon.

"I understand that you're here to ask me about my exhusband," she began. "I'm willing to talk to you only because if I refuse, you're bound to think that I know something of interest about his death. I'd rather talk to you and get it over with than have somebody digging around in my personal life. I want that to be very clear. This is the first and last time we will talk....So now, tell me who you are, and what you want to know about my ex-husband."

Héctor handed her his license and waited for her to return it to him.

"I'm looking for something in your husband's past that might explain why he was killed. Maybe if you could tell me…"

"Gaspar was an upstart, a social climber. He married me for my money and my family's prestige. Our marriage was just another couple of steps up the ladder of his career. I made a mistake and I paid for it. Now I'm free."

"Is there anything in his past…Any unusual relationships? Financial problems? Something from when he was younger?"

"He was an upstart, a hustler, a loner, without friends, few acquaintances. He never had problems with money—as a matter of fact, he was overly cautious. He was very clever, you know, but rose slowly through the ranks…I don't know what I could tell you that could be of any help."

Héctor listened in silence. It didn't feel right, there was something missing from the picture. The woman stood up, and Héctor had no choice but to do the same. She led him to the door.

"I'm sorry I couldn't help you more."

"Not as sorry as I am. I apologize for wasting your time."

Héctor headed out through the garden, leaving the woman in the doorway.

"There's one thing, Detective."

Héctor turned his head.

"It might help you to know that my ex-husband was a homosexual."

Back at the Carousel Cinema, he turned the new piece of information over in his mind. He bought some fried meat and tortillas and assembled his tacos while he watched the people entering the theater. No one of interest showed up for the second show.

He got back into his car and set out toward Marisa Ferrer's Florida neighborhood. His breath tasted sour in his mouth, his neck hurt from sleeping in the armchair at the office, and traffic was backed up along Insurgentes all the way to the Hotel de Mexico. He wished someone conducting an opinion poll would get in the car and ask him a few questions. He'd tell them he didn't have the slightest idea why he'd become a detective.

The maid opened the door and let him in without asking any questions.

Marisa Ferrer was waiting for him in the living room.

"Any word?" the detective asked.

"No. I talked to some friends of mine in the police department, but they didn't know where to start." She hadn't cried, but she appeared extremely tense, like a fighting cock ready to attack.

"I want to ask you something. It's something that could be very important in helping me find your daughter, so listen carefully and think about it before you give me your answer. Is there anything that you've hidden from Elena that she could have found out about lately?"

She hesitated momentarily.

"My lovers…"

"Have there been very many?"

"That's a private matter."

The tension increased between them.

"Are you sure there's not something else?"

"I don't think so."

"Do any of your daughter's friends ever come over here?"

"She was going out with a boy named Arturo up until a couple of months ago. He would come by, and a few of her girlfriends from school…"

"Anyone named Esteban?"

She thought for a minute.

"Esteban, no, not that I remember."

"Where did she go when she went out with her friends?"

"To the movies, or to one of those hamburger places out on Insurgentes. Like all the kids these days…She used to go to the bowling alley a lot until she broke up with Arturo. But then later on she started going there again on her own."

"This *Señor* Burgos I met here the other day…"

"You didn't like him, did you?"

Héctor shook his head.

"That's unfortunate. He's an old family friend."

"Is that all?"

She didn't answer. She sat fingering the stitching on a pillow on the couch, playing with it. Then she started to cry.

Héctor left the room and headed straight for the door. He didn't like the situation one bit. It irked him that he had waited so long before trying to figure out where Elena had met Es. and G. (it sounded like a brand of Scotch).

They had come into the picture after the 50,000-peso-what-ever-it-was, in response to Elena's request to help her get rid of it.

Why was there a case of soda pop in the back of their car?

He turned and went back into the living room. Marisa Ferrer had stopped crying, and now sat staring straight ahead.

"Which bowling alley?"

"The Florida Bowl, a few blocks from here."

He decided to skip the third showing of the movie. Old Man Zapata wasn't likely to be out so late. The night was warm and pleasant. Héctor thought he heard the wings of a bird flutter overhead. He leaned against the car, smoking. Then he walked slowly to the pay phone at the corner.

"Is Elisa there?…Elisa? Can you do me a favor? But you're going to think it's kind of strange. I want you to go talk with a forensic specialist and ask him if an engineer named Osorio Barba who was murdered a couple of months ago was a homosexual…Talk to the guy who did the autopsy for the police… Give him some money, and I'll pay you back."

He hung up. Now was the time to stir things up, but how? First he tried the drive-ins along Insurgentes. They'd done a good business once, when the kids had hung out there in their fast cars and drag-raced along the strip. But now they were just shadows of what they'd once been, converted into middle-class watering holes, filled with kids out for their first solo drive, flirtatious packs of teenage girls, and bored waiters. No sign of Greenjacket or Armgrabber. He didn't remember much at all about the third one. He had a vague picture of a fat boy with curly hair, but he hadn't ever gotten a good look at him.

He drove out toward Navarte, as far as Luz Saviñón, and stopped in front of a modest middle-class home. A moving van was pulled up to the door.

"Is the maid around?"

"She went home days ago. The owner's cleared the place out."

"The owner?"

"Yeah, the engineer's brother. I work with him at the mattress factory…"

"Mind if I take a look around?" Héctor showed his license.

"Go ahead. But there's hardly anything left."

Héctor inspected the abandoned house. It looked as if it had been hit by a tornado, furniture scattered about recklessly, everything packed up hurriedly and without affection.

In the bedroom there was nothing but the mattress leaning against one wall, the bed dismantled, an empty closet, two pictures lying on the floor.

It was past ten o'clock. He thanked the mover and walked outside to his car. He pulled a small notebook from his pocket and tried to organize his thoughts, only to lose himself in a hodgepodge of names and facts.

"When are the three stories going to come together?" he wondered, half joking, half waiting for an answer.

What about Burgos? What did he know about him? Nothing, except that he didn't like his face…Him and a few thousand other people whose looks Héctor didn't like.

There was always the bowling alley and the case of soda pop. Those two seemed to go together, offering a possible answer to the question of where Elena met Es. and G.

Then there was Marisa Ferrer dissolving into tears. Not a very convincing sight. What was she hiding?

There was one gay engineer, dead, and another engineer named Camposanto who could invite him to a party, according to the fat worker in the *lonchería*.

There was also Rodríguez Cuesta's strange, unaccountable un
easiness. And the increasingly militant conflict with the union.

Plus Alvarez Cerruli's predecessor in death, a corpse named
Bravo Osorio Barba. Was he a homosexual, too?

There was a girlfriend named Bustamante, and a boyfriend
named Arturo.

The ex-wife of the dead engineer, a maid who'd already gone
home to her village, a lawyer named Duelas, a tall, dark-haired
independent union leader, and a scab in a tan suit from the
pro-government federation.

And three men that had gotten passports through the Mexican Embassy in Costa Rica in 1934.

If that wasn't enough, there was also a mysterious shoe box
with papers from old man Belascoarán, Héctor's father, and a
wad of letters sitting in his pocket he hadn't had a chance to read.

And he had to buy the soda for the office, do his laundry,
keep on living his life.

He'd started the list as a joke, but by the end, he felt completely overwhelmed. In order of priorities, he ought to start with
the bowling alley, but he opted for the least important instead,
remembering his old buddy El Cuervo Valdivia on the radio.

XEFS broadcast from the offices of Radio One Thousand,
on Insurgentes, in the Florida district, and after wandering for
awhile through a maze of hallways and studios, Héctor found
the room where El Cuervo did his show every night from eleven
o'clock until dawn. But El Cuervo hadn't arrived yet, so, shaking
off his fatigue, Héctor decided to quit procrastinating and go
investigate The Florida Bowl.

Was he afraid?

He'd been afraid often enough to know what it felt like.
But very seldom had he felt fear of physical violence; mostly it
had been a fear of loneliness, fear of responsibility, of making a
mistake. This particular feeling was different. It was more like
the combination of fear and fatigue. Not a bad state of mind
for a man about to enter combat, he thought.

The din of rolling balls and falling pins slapped him across the face like the crest of a wave. He looked around for the pair of faces he wanted to see—from table to table, among the groups of bowlers, in the kitchen behind the revolving door, inside the office, and at the front desk where the cashier was passing out shoes and score sheets.

Nothing. He walked slowly to the counter.

What was he supposed to say?

He decided to take the direct route.

"I'm looking for a girl named Elena," he said, staring sternly at the overweight man smiling behind the counter.

"Never heard of her."

"She's been kidnapped."

"Oh yeah?" said the fat man, smiling.

"I'd like permission to search the premises."

"Wish I could help you, buddy. Only I can't, so get lost."

"If that's how you want it." Héctor decided not to push it. He turned his back on the fat man and made his way slowly toward the exit. When he reached the door, he turned around again and traded stares with the fat man who sat serenely behind the cash register. After a while, the fat man raised his hand in the air and gave Héctor the finger. Héctor made a motion as if he were playing a violin, and walked out into the night.

He was very, very tired.

# Chapter Six

*Later on I understood that the tangos lied,*
*but by then it was much too late.*

—Mario Benedetti

"…so we grabbed the Hunchback of Notre Dame and tried to chain him up…but then he really starts to wail on us, I mean like it wasn't a game anymore."

"You remember Rosas? Short guy, kind of dark…with hair like a bird? He thought he was such a tough guy. Well, he's walking along and then this hand comes right out of the wall at him…"

"The hairy hand!"

"He pissed in his pants, the little shit pissed right in his pants."

"You remember that guy Echenique? Well he comes down off that bridge they had there, this real funky, scary old bridge, he comes down off the bridge and this old lady jumps on him shouting all about how she's La Llorona, and asking him if he was one of her kids. He flew out of there like a bat out of hell, you should have seen it, man. So then he comes over to us and he wants us to go back with him and cop a feel on the old bag, so we all run down there and La Llorona keeps screaming about how we're all her long-lost children and all this shit, and so one of the guys gets his hand up her skirt…and it's a guy!"

"I was going around with some of the kids from my class, and we were feeling pretty cool, until this mummy pops out of his coffin and grabs one of our guys, and won't let him go. 'I didn't do nothing, lemme go,' the guy says, and the mummy tells him, 'You broke into the pyramid and pillaged my tomb.' 'It wasn't me, it wasn't me,' the guy screams. Man, I was never so scared in my life. I mean, it seems pretty funny now, but back then I was scared shitless. What was it called? Just 'The Haunted

House,' or something like that, I guess. In that construction site on Insurgentes."

"It was the scariest thing I ever saw."

"We loved it back then," said Belascoarán.

They sat together in a tiny room. Records lined the walls. Valdivia had a bottle of rum, and was drinking an improvised *cuba libre* from a paper cup. Héctor drank ginger ale, savoring the taste in his mouth.

"So what are you doing now?" Valdivia asked at last.

"I'm a detective."

"With the cops?"

"No. Independent." He didn't like the sound of "private detective." "Independent" had a much better ring to it.

"I remember hearing that you got a degree in engineering."

"Yeah."

"And then?"

Instead of retelling the story he'd left behind, Héctor described the strange triangle of mysteries he was involved in now. With one corner in Delex Inc. and the dead engineer. One in the shining eyes and the myth of *don* Emiliano Zapata. And the other in the story of a scared teenage girl with her arm in a cast.

Valdivia sat lost in thought.

"I heard you on the radio the other night. I liked your show a lot. But, you know, sometimes I thought you were almost too nice to people, you pander to your audience too much. Almost like you're trying to sell them something."

"What time were you listening?"

"From about ten until twelve-thirty, something like that."

"That's just when things are starting to heat up. Later on the listeners do it all."

There was another brief silence.

"Do you want me to lend a hand?" asked the disc jockey.

"With what?"

"Oh, I don't know…Just if you get into any trouble you could give me a call. I'll put it on the radio, and the folks out there'll do what they can. You can't imagine how many people are out there listening just waiting for the chance to help out, to be part of something. There's so many people in this town who either want to help somebody else, or need help themselves."

"I believe you."

"Keep it in mind. I'll give you our phone numbers. There's six of them, use any one." He held out a card.

"It's great seeing you again."

"It's been a long time. Good luck." They hugged and Héctor went out into the hall.

Valdivia turned to look at him. He was extremely thin, balding, and with an enormous mustache and clear eyes.

"Whatever you want, just let me know. Who knows, it might spark up the show a little bit."

Belascoarán headed out toward Camposanto's house in Napoles. He turned on the radio.

*An old friend of mine came by to visit me tonight. Isn't it unbelievable how easy it is to lose track of people in this town? The city just swallows them up. Well, I'll tell you, it was a real pleasure seeing this guy again. These days he's working as a detective, an independent investigator, you could say, and he promised to call in every once in a while and let us know how it's going. We'll see if we can't give him a hand.*

*Now I'm going to spin you all a tune by Cuco Sánchez. It's called 'Arrieros Somos,' and if you think about it, it just might make a good theme song for this program, a good way to start out the long, hard night.*

*You're listening to the El Cuervo Show on XEFS. The lines are open, at 511-22-47, 511-31-19, 587-87-21, 566-45-65, 544-31-27, and 568-89-43. This is El Cuervo, your partner in the night, your bridge through the darkness. Mobilizing the city's wasted resources, forging a road of solidarity for the denizens of the night, for all you vampires out there…Don't be afraid, don't be ashamed. Everybody has problems, and the easy answers are few and far between.*

The hoarse, melancholy voice of Cuco Sánchez burst from the stereo speakers:

> *Arrieros somos*
> *y el el camino andamos...*
> (We are mule drivers
> out on the open road...)

Belascoarán parked fifty yards back from Camposanto's building, on the same side of the street. He got out and walked up to the garage. The engineer's car wasn't there. More time wasted. He cursed his bad luck.

The bright neon lights, even the traffic signals, hurt his eyes. He winced. His shirt collar had the consistency of wet cardboard, and his socks felt like a macaroni salad oozing around his toes. It seemed like a good time to call it quits, but with stubborn determination, Héctor pointed the car toward the south side of town. He stopped in a gas station, gassed up the car, and took a leak.

The lights were out in The Florida Bowl. Héctor peered through the thick glass of the front door, but he couldn't see a thing. He inspected the two apartment buildings that stood on either side, and then took a walk around the block. The streets were empty, except for a pair of lovers he passed on one corner, but they hadn't even looked at him. Behind the bowling alley, on the other side of the block, was a grocery store. Héctor walked the block again, hoping to find some opening to slip through. Finally, he tried the garage of one of the adjacent apartment buildings.

The door had been left unlocked, with its padlock fastened uselessly to a chain at the side. Héctor stepped in. After tripping over a garbage can and surprising a stray cat, he came across a low green door, about three feet high, that let into the wall on the bowling alley side. He pulled back the squeaky bolt and opened the door to find four steps leading down into a lowceilinged basement. He ducked inside and made his way, stooping, among the junk cast off from the bowling alley, until he got to a stockpile of chipped and broken balls. He could feel the nicks in the otherwise perfect spheres. He continued on in the total darkness, guiding himself with one hand on the wall.

He tripped twice over some wooden poles lying on the floor, then took out his lighter and lit it briefly to orient himself. At the opposite end from where he'd entered there was another rusty door. He approached it. It had no lock, but was held shut by a simple bolt on the other side.

He checked his pockets for something he could use to slide the bolt back, knowing he didn't have anything. He searched around with the lighter until it burned his fingers, but there was nothing among the wasted lumber and splintered pins, broken barrel slats and assorted garbage that covered the floor. He retraced his steps back to where he'd come in, tripping several times in the darkness. Each time it made him wish he'd gone into broadcasting, or maybe the priesthood instead. He emerged into the street rubbing his ankle where it had been attacked by the fender of one of the cars parked in the garage. What at first had seemed like a simple exercise was turning into an major expedition. But he was a craftsman, after all. Hadn't he said it himself?

In the glove compartment of the car, he found a long, thin screwdriver, and then returned to the garage. The street remained empty. He passed through the door once again and, remembering the path between the piles of discarded lumber, made his way to the door at the far end. He found the jamb and started to work on the bolt. On the third try he got it to slide back into its sleeve, and the door opened, creaking, into the darkness. Groping his way slowly, he climbed a set of stairs similar to the ones at the other end. But not anticipating the extra step, he tripped and fell, spraining his right wrist. At that point he distinguished a dim light ahead of him and dropped carefully to the ground.

Very slowly, he reached for his gun, trying at the same time to suppress the rhythmic sound of the air escaping his lungs. He could hear a pair of voices, and receding footsteps.

"…What's he gonna do? Nothing. He doesn't know a thing. He's just shooting in the dark coming around here. But all the same, it's better if you guys stay away for a few days, and take her with you. I don't want her around here anymore. I've got a buddy who manages a hotel out on Zaragoza Boulevard. I gave Gerónimo the address. We can keep her there until this thing cools out a little…"

*Say the name of the hotel, say the name of the hotel, dammit.*

"Why don't I just teach the dude a little lesson? I'll wait for him out front the next time he comes around and…"

The voices and the footsteps moved farther away. By tilting his head, Héctor tried to look through the grating at the bottom of the door that led into the bowling alley proper, but all he saw was a pair of black boots that clicked against the floor and disappeared. He tried to guess where he was. Were they walking in the direction of the kitchen?

Carefully, he made his way back until he was sitting in his car once again. He lit a cigarette and tried to think.

When he went in, there hadn't been any cars with people in them in the street. The same three empty cars were still parked where he'd last seen them. But while he'd been in the basement, a car from somewhere had apparently come for Elena, who had presumably left with the man talking to the fellow in the black boots. Héctor got out of the car and walked across to the garage of the apartment building on the other side. They could have left from there. And if they'd been there when he first drove up, then they must have seen him. And so while he was crawling around in the basement, they'd gone and gotten the girl out of the bowling alley and put her in their car.

It was too farfetched.

Do you spell Gerónimo with a *G* or a *J*?

How many hotels were there on Zaragoza Boulevard?

No, it couldn't be, it all seemed too easy. He was letting himself be fooled.

For one thing, he'd dropped in on the conversation at exactly the right moment. He didn't like easy answers. There was no such thing as a lucky break in a city of twelve million people. The only luck there was was bad luck.

It could all be a trick they were laying for him, expecting him to fall for it, like a dummy.

He started the car, and drove a couple of blocks away from The Florida Bowl, parking in front of a house where there was a party going on. The music, the smell of food, and the bright lights poured through the windows of the house.

A strange idea suddenly popped into Héctor's head: What if Elena hadn't been kidnapped at all? Marisa Ferrer's tears had given him the impression of someone letting water out of a tap.

He had three possibilities to choose from: Go back and beat the answer out of the guy with the black boots; see if he could get any more information out of Marisa Ferrer; or try to check out the two-hundred-plus hotels there must be on Zaragoza Boulevard.

A fourth alternative was to go home and get some sleep. The temptation was great, and growing rapidly by the minute. But prompted by a vague sense of duty, plus the thought of the girl with her arm in a cast, he decided to put off sleep a while longer. He rubbed his eyes with the palms of his hands, and lit another cigarette. The taste of the tobacco nauseated him, and he threw it out the window, sucking in the fresh night air. He started up the car, pulled out, and turned on the radio. The wind in his face made him feel better.

> *If you're not feeling too with it, brother, don't let it get you down. It's not your fault. After all, it's two o'clock in the morning, and maybe you didn't sleep so good.*
>
> *You're listening to the El Cuervo Show, solidarity radio, going out to all the stray dogs and vampires roaming the nocturnal landscape of this desolate city. To all you folks out there working overtime, students cramming for tomorrow's exam, late-night truckers, strikers on guard duty, hookers, luckless crooks, independent detectives, frustrated lovers, lonely hearts, recidivist loners, and other types of nocturnal fauna.*
>
> *Let El Cuervo be your guide and companion, the magical raven of the eternal night, ready to lend a*

*[handwritten marginal note: doesn't include the rich & the wealthy]*

*hand where help is needed. Before we listen to a pair
of sambas from Brazil, I want to give everybody this
urgent message. Señor Valdez at one seventeen Gabino
Barreda, apartment number three hundred and one,
in San Rafael, called in to say that the pipes burst in
the bathroom of his apartment and the place is filling
up with water. He's got a flood on his hands. Anybody
who lives in the neighborhood, he needs buckets and
people to help out.*

*I hope that Señor Valdez gives us a call later on to
let us know how it's going and how many people show
up to lend a hand.*

*Now, a pair of Brazilian love songs from Joao Gil-
berto to keep you company in the night.*

The music flooded into the car. For five minutes Héctor had
been driving around and around the block, unsure whether to
stick with his earlier plan or to go out to San Rafael and help
*Señor* Valdez.

"Time to take the bull by the horns," he told himself, trying
to sound convincing. But the seriousness of his resolve was
undercut by another yawn. If things kept up like this he was
going to end up with a deformed jawbone.

He headed for the actress's house. The car seemed to drive
itself, dropping him in front of the two-story building.

He rang the bell repeatedly, until the maid finally opened the
door a crack. Héctor pushed the door back and stepped inside.
The maid didn't move. An old robe hung over her shoulders,
with a white cotton nightgown underneath. Then without a
word, she stepped aside to let Héctor pass. He moved through
the hallway, opening doors. What was he so angry for? What
made him think the actress had tricked him?

All of a sudden it occurred to him that Marisa Ferrer might
have company in bed with her, and he stopped dead in front of
the door he assumed led to her bedroom. He knocked lightly
with his knuckles, there was no answer, and he opened the door.
A single lamp illuminated the room where the actress, who had

climbed the hard road to the top, lay sleeping, face-down under the pearl-gray sheets, her bare shoulders showing, and her arms resting awkwardly at her sides. Belascoarán crossed to the bed and touched her, but the woman didn't respond. She lay still, as the detective's hand shook her gently.

He glanced around at the maid who stood wordlessly in the doorway, watching him, pulling her robe firmly around her with her arms crossed over her chest.

"Has she been like this before?"

The maid nodded.

He opened the drawer of the nightstand. Inside were a syringe and an envelope of white powder. He threw them back into the drawer and slammed it shut violently, then stormed out of the house, with the maid following him to the door.

The outside air cooled his anger, and he climbed back into the car, determined to break the impasse. The radio let out a rhythmic African beat.

He stopped again in front of The Florida Bowl. There was always the possibility of turning a trap around to catch the ones who had set it. But how many hotels could there be on Zaragoza Boulevard? He could remember at least a dozen right off the bat, and that was without thinking very hard. There must be at least forty, minimum. And how to find the one the girl was being kept in? If they'd really been trying to lure him into a trap they would have said which hotel it was. The whole scheme was too elaborate otherwise.

Héctor got out of the car and walked back through the door in the garage, following the route he'd pioneered a few hours earlier. There was a certain tenacity, a certain stubbornness that made him go on, forsaking sleep, placing one foot in front of the other on his long trek through the endless night.

Once past the second door, with the humid air of the basement behind him, he tried to orient himself inside the open space of the bowling alley. The tables and lanes were to the right, the kitchen was at the back and to the left, and the living quarters were probably beyond that. He headed carefully in that direction, until he came to a door with a dim circle of light escaping around the jamb. Rubbing his sleepy eyes, he drew his gun, then kicked angrily at the door.

One of the hinges broke, sending splinters flying, and leaving the door to hang crazily askew on the bottom hinge.

A single lamp lit the room, where the fat man lay on his bed reading a *fotonovela*. His boots stood nearby, freshly shined. There were a couple of glasses on a night table, along with a half-empty bottle of Pepsi and a package of cough drops. On a chair, a wrinkled pair of pants and a switchblade. There was a bookshelf with a bundle of old newspapers tied with string, and two packs of Philip Morris that reminded him of the conference room at Delex. A soccer poster and a pair of Lin May pinups hung on the wall.

The fat man dropped his comic book and retreated to the farthest corner of the bed.

"*Buenas noches,*" Héctor deadpanned.

The fat man didn't make a sound.

Héctor took another glance around the squalid little room. What the hell was he supposed to do now? It had all seemed so simple: take out your gun, kick the door down, rush into the room. Now, according to the script, he ought to either beat the shit out of the fat man until he gave the name of the hotel on Zaragoza Boulevard, or lure him into a conversation and trick him into spilling the beans that way.

Héctor didn't feel capable of either one, so he simply stood there in silence.

They remained like that for a couple of minutes while Héctor tried to think of a way out. What if he tied the guy up, waited outside for him to free himself, and then followed him? Or what if he allowed him to make a phone call, and intercepted the call? That one made him smile. How the hell do you intercept a phone call in Mexico City?

The fat man returned Héctor's smile.

"What's so funny?" Héctor demanded. He was feeling more uncomfortable by the minute.

"Nothing."

They spent another couple of minutes without speaking, and the fat man started to grow visibly more nervous.

Héctor couldn't think of anything else to do, so he jumped up onto the bed. The mattress sank under his weight, and he gracefully jumped back to where he'd been standing a moment before. Horrified, the fat man rolled off onto the floor.

Héctor turned his back on the fat man and left the room.

There were one hundred seventeen hotels and motels on Zaragoza Boulevard listed in the directory. Héctor felt like crying. But instead, he gathered his dirty clothes to send them out to be washed, piled his dirty dishes in the sink, emptied and washed the ashtrays, opened the windows, and dropped, fully dressed, onto his bed. "Life sucks," he mumbled. But in spite of his fatigue he couldn't sleep. At five A.M. he jumped out of bed, stuck his head under the cold-water tap, and held it there for several minutes. He was overwhelmed by a tremendous feeling of defeat.

LA TOLVANERA, read the weatherbeaten sign by the roadside. Héctor stowed his book in his jacket pocket and walked toward the village's deserted streets. He'd been traveling for fifteen straight hours, combining sleep with the restful contemplation of the broken and eroded plains beyond Huajapan de León.

The town was made up of four dusty, windblown streets. It looked dead. The detective walked into a *lonchería*, La Rosita— PEPSI COLA ES MEJOR, their sign said—to escape the wind. He paused to let his eyes grow accustomed to the shadowy interior. An old man stood behind the counter.

"Excuse me, can you tell me where I could find *don* Eladio Huerta?"

"He passed away."

"Did he leave any family?"

"Didn't have any."

"How long ago did he die?"

"Three years. The cemetery's on up the road another hundred yards or so."

Belascoarán went back outside. There was a parts house at the outer edge of town, where a couple of men worked in the dust kicked up by an old cattle truck.

"*Buen día.*"

"*Buenos días.*" That was one of the nice things about a small town. People still said hello to one another.

Past the parts house was a wrecking yard, and past that, the open plain where the cemetery sat: fifty graves with their worm-eaten crosses, and the dry grass growing all around.

ELADIO HUERTA 1882–1973.

There was a yellowed photograph under the name.

That was it, another dead end. Now there was nothing to do but go back and face the city again. Go back and spend another night in front of the engineer's house, and search 117 hotels for a kidnapped girl. The whole trip had been a wild-goose chase.

He walked back out to the highway and stood for a couple of hours, fighting against the brutal wind that swept across the isthmus from the Pacific to the Atlantic. A second-class bus picked him up and continued lamely on its way toward Oaxaca.

The bus from Oaxaca got into Mexico City at 2:10 in the morning, and a battered detective climbed down after thirty-five hours of continuous travel. He found his car where he had left it parked in front of the terminal, and headed down Insurgentes. The radio kept him company.

> *Whatever you've been waiting for, wait no more. And if you've already given up hope that what you're waiting for will ever come, then rest assured you did the right thing. Consider yourself the absolute master over the days and hours ahead of you. Quit crying in front of the mirror, make yourself a strong cup of coffee and smile. Don't ask questions.*
>
> *The night is your friend...*

A Peter, Paul and Mary song came over the radio, reminding Héctor of earlier days, when each week was spent in anticipation of Saturday night.

He stopped in front of The Florida Bowl, and looked around until he found what he was looking for in a construction site farther down the street: chunks of broken brick. He lugged about twenty pounds of projectiles over to the bowling alley, and started to hurl them rapid-fire at the windows, under the neon glow of the streetlights. The glass burst into a million pieces in front of his eyes, and all of a sudden he discovered he was having fun. He tossed the last few bricks, glanced quickly over his handiwork, jumped back into his car, and was gone before the lights started to come on in the neighboring apartments.

"He just laughed. I felt like such an idiot. I swear, the kind of things you find for me to do…"

Elisa dedicated herself to the plate of spaghetti in front of her. She ate voraciously, but with style.

"He asked me if I thought that two months after the guy died they could still stick a light up his asshole and figure out his sexual preferences. He laughed at me."

Héctor couldn't keep from smiling.

"What'd you do then?"

"I told him to go to hell and left. It's a terrible place there… *Ay nanita*…they've got the bodies stacked up like cases of beer in a truck."

"Well, thanks, all the same."

Elisa renewed her attack on the plate of spaghetti, while Héctor, who wasn't hungry, watched her eat. They were sitting in a sidewalk cafe in the *Zona Rosa* on a beautiful, sunny afternoon.

"But wait, there's more…"

"More?" asked Héctor, pleasantly distracted by a pair of slender dark legs two tables away. The brilliant sunshine warmed his bones.

"Since you weren't around, I decided to go ahead on my own." She paused for another mouthful.

"Do they eat a lot of Italian food in Canada?"

"Plenty," she said with her mouth full.

"It's pretty popular?"

"Uh-huh."

The black woman at the other table glanced over at Héctor, and then turned her attention back to the menu.

"What'd you say about doing something on your own?" he asked.

Elisa mopped her plate with a piece of bread, then let the waiter take it away. In its place he left a double order of squid in its ink, with rice.

"I'm so hungry I could eat…"

"What'd you find out?"

"This guy Osorio Barba was a real loner. No family, very self-seeking, just a gray guy with a reputation as an experienced engineer. There wasn't anyone in his building who had more than a couple of words to say about him. Until I talked to the doorman."

Enjoying the rhythm of their conversation, she turned her attention to the plate of squid. She was a thin, broad-shouldered woman, who inherited her freckles and red hair from the Irish side of the family. Recovering from an early marriage to a Canadian journalist who turned out to be a paranoid alcoholic, she was just now starting to get her feet back on the ground after four years away from home. She and Héctor shared a love of the unexpected, and for staying up all night. She played the guitar passably well, and wrote poetry she never showed to anyone else. "I'm a train on a dead-end line," she said about herself.

"How is it?"

"*Buenísimo, buenísimo.* Do you want to try some?"

Héctor shook his head, and then, as always, changed his mind. He took his fork and fished a giant piece of squid off Elisa's plate.

"The doorman sold me a box of papers from the dead man's apartment. It cost me a hundred pesos, but the only thing worth-while was a piece of paper with three names and addresses stuck inside a folder full of invoices from the factory."

"And then?"

"I went and checked them out. They're all middle-class boys, between about twenty and twenty-five years old, two of them are students, one's an accountant at the Banco de Commercio. I'll cut my eyelashes if they're not all gay."

"Let me see the names."

"First pay me the hundred pesos they cost me."

Héctor took a bill out of his pocket.

"Come on, Héctor, lighten up. I was only kidding."

Héctor smiled.

"Is it going to help you any?"

"I don't know, not really. All it does, is it seems to show that now there's two dead gay engineers instead of one."

"Just imagine what the tabloids could do with that one: 'Homicidal Den of Queer Executives Exposed in Santa Clara!'"

The waiter approached their table.

"Can I get you anything else?"

"How about a piece of strawberry pie?"

He brought a papaya *licuado* up from the juice bar downstairs and was sipping at it slowly while he gazed out the window toward the gray office buildings across the street, their own dirty windows masking whatever went on inside. A few lights started to come on.

Belascoarán picked up the phone book and looked for the number for The Florida Bowl. He dialed the seven digits.

"Hello. Florida Bowl."

He let a few seconds pass by.

"Listen here, fatty, I've got this funny idea about burning down a little hotel on Zaragoza Boulevard, and then tossing a few sticks of dynamite into that lousy dump of yours."

He could hear the sound of balls striking pins in the background.

"Tell your buddies to tune into radio station XEFS to-night."

He hung up.

"What's going on, neighbor?"

"*Don* Gilberto. How's it going?"

"Where've you been lately? I did that job you asked me to do."

"Let's hear it."

"The old man who lived in Olivar de los Padres was a real quiet guy who used to keep pretty much to himself. He braided horse leads and sold them for a living. Sometimes the kids from the local soccer team would visit him, and they'd sit around and talk. He got a veteran's pension, fought with Zapata in the Revolution. Had a reputation for being a feisty old guy. Ten years ago, when the *granaderos* came in to boot the squatters out of the neighborhood, he comes out of his house with an old carbine and lets go with a few rounds. He split for good in 1970. Didn't leave a forwarding address. They say he went away once a long time ago, too, but after a while he came back. There's no one living in the house now, the squatters use it as a place to store construction materials."

He waited for Héctor's response, but the detective just listened in silence, doodling flowers on an old newspaper on his desk.

"That's all she wrote. I've got to be going now. Got a real sweet little job waiting for me."

"Whose plumbing are you going to play with tonight?" Héctor smiled.

"Professional secrets, old buddy, professional secrets. Want me to turn on the light for you?"

Héctor shook his head.

He took the bunch of letters he'd been carrying around in his coat pocket for the last few days and added them to the stack of mail piling up on his desk. Then he sat down in the old swivel chair and propped his feet up on the desktop. Despite the lengthening shadows, he could still see the three photos tacked to the wall.

*Don* Emiliano, the corpse sprawled across the desk, and the girl with her arm wrapped in plaster. Who was pursuing whom? The night dropped vertically over the city.

He stood up and turned his attention back to the list of hotels on Zaragoza Boulevard. Now it was just a question of patience.

"Give me the manager. That's right, the manager…Listen, mister, tell your buddies they've got until midnight tonight to free the girl, otherwise I'm going to blow your hotel to smithereens."

He hung up.

It was going to take a hell of a long time to get through the whole list. And what if they'd been talking about a hotel near the boulevard, and not directly on it?

After an hour and a half he'd managed to make about seventy-five calls. Each one brought the same response: Who is it? Who's calling? Curses or wisecracks. It could be the first one he'd called, or it could be the last. He kept on doggedly. His mouth was getting dry.

"I want to talk to the manager…with the night clerk, then… Hello? Tell your friends they've got until midnight tonight to let the girl go or I'm going to blow up the hotel. Don't give me any of that shit."

He hung up.

"What's this about blowing up hotels? And whatcha doin' in here with the lights out?" asked the sewer expert, arriving for the start of his night's work.

"I want to talk to the manager…Hello? Tell your buddies they've got until midnight tonight to let the girl go, if not I'll blow your fucking hotel into a million pieces."

He crossed the Hotel del Peregrino off the list. Next: Hotel del Monte.

"Temporary insanity. I'm prone to these attacks every now and then. Didn't you know?"

"You're hoarse. You been doing this a long time?"

"A couple of hours."

"I'll spell you awhile. What do I have to say?"

Héctor told him the rap and handed him the telephone, pointing to the place on the list where he'd left off. Then he went over to the secret compartment and took out a soda pop. The last one. Dammit, he'd been ragging on the plumber and now he'd forgotten himself. They would give him hell for that one.

"I want to talk to the manager right away, it's very important," El Gallo spoke into the telephone. "Listen, asshole, tell your buddies they've got until midnight tonight to let the girl go, 'cause if they don't I'm going to wipe your lousy flophouse off the map. I've got the dynamite right here."

He hung up.

"How'd I do?"

"Not so hot. Better let me do it."

"Let me do it awhile, will ya? I kind of get a kick out of it."

Héctor slumped into the armchair.

"The only thing is, neighbor, I can't see worth shit here in the dark. Do you think we could turn the lights on?"

"Sorry, Gallo, I've got a headache, that's all."

He got up, turned on the lights, and went back to his armchair.

"Give me the manager…Listen, you damn son of a bitch, you and your friends have until exactly midnight tonight to give up the girl. If not, I'm going to blow your lousy hotel to kingdom come."

The engineer looked absolutely radiant.

Héctor turned his attention to the mail on his desk. The first piece was a telegram:

> ADDRESS SUPPLIED CORRESPONDS TO HOUSE DEMOL-
> ISHED 16 YEARS AGO. OWNER KILLED IN TRAFFIC
> ACCIDENT. GARZA HERNÁNDEZ AGENCY. MONTERREY.

That took care of the three passports issued in San José, Costa Rica.

"…your lousy hotel to smithereens."

A note for a registered package of books mailed from Guadalajara. He put it aside.

A letter from the Mexican Academy of Criminal Investigation, inviting him to give a course on whatever topic he wanted. He threw it away.

A letter from the Kai Feng School of Karate and Martial Arts, with an illustrated folder detailing courses and fees. A letter to

Gilberto from a *Señora* Saenz de Mier, complaining that, thanks to him, her shower now leaked rusty water and the toilet filled with soap bubbles when she flushed it.

He put it aside as a keepsake. All that was left was for her to hear the French National Anthem when she took a piss, he mused.

"…two sticks of dynamite and your hotel's gonna be history, buddy. Ha ha ha!" El Gallo had made some distinct improvements on Héctor's original message.

Two more pieces of junk mail, one from a toy store, the other for an art show.

A special mail-order offer for a complete set of "Seventh Circle" mystery novels, 215 volumes, 2000 pesos.

Not a bad price, he thought.

"Hello? I want to talk to the manager…"

At the bottom of the pile, as if waiting for the less important things to be cleared away first, lay a pair of letters covered with strange stamps and postmarks. He considered whether to open them then and there, or to relegate them once again to his coat pocket, until the affair of the 117 hotels was satisfactorily completed.

For the time being he felt a stronger obligation to the Ferrer girl than to this woman with the ponytail who was at once so near and so far away. But when he thought about it, it seemed to him that his disastrous love life fit quite well into the three-pronged labyrinth he was caught up in. Hey, not a bad title for a detective novel, he thought, *The Three-Pronged Labyrinth*, by Héctor Belascoarán Shayne.

He lit a cigarette.

"We won't think twice about blowing the dump sky high. Believe me, buddy, I've got the dynamite right here…"

It would make a good detective story, if it weren't for the fact that he was sitting right in the middle of it already, if he weren't so caught up in the role in which he'd been cast.

He opened the first letter:

I guess your letters must be following me out there somewhere. I hope you don't think I'm running away from them, it's just that I've picked up the pace, and these days I'm moving faster than the light that comes from Mexico. How would you like to stay in a different hotel every night? Doesn't that sound wonderful? Fortunately, my money's running out, and of course, I'm not going to ask my father for even one cent. Some time soon I'll have to decide if I want to burn my bridges and spend the money I was saving in reserve, and start a new kind of trek, as a sort of Mexican hobo loose in Europe; or if I want to decide that the trip is over and I can go home to Mexico.

Either way, I've got ten dollars set aside to send you a telegram letting you know what I'm going to do.

How are you, *mi amor*?

Same as before? My lonely little puppy dog? I've been seeing you a lot lately. My shrink back in Mexico would say that I'm exhibiting symptoms of paranoia. Yesterday I saw you on the ferryboat in the Bosporus, and last week you were in a shepherds' bar in Albania, and just the other day, on the sports page of *France Soir*. I swear it. Your doubles, your alter egos, are following me all over Europe.

I suppose they're out chasing stranglers just like you, or maybe they've only come out to witness my misbehavings.

How do you spell *solución*? With an *s* or *c*?

I love you even as I run from you. I wait for you every night in my empty bed, and in my dreams.

—ME

"...If they don't give her up, I'm going to blow that lousy hotel of yours sky high. Yeah, it's that bad, buddy. So hurry up."

Included in the letter was a photograph of the woman wit the ponytail, on a boat, leaning on the handrail, and looking out over the sea with a half smile lighting up her face. Her hair blew in the wind, she wore a plaid skirt, stockings, and a sheen blouse.

The second letter was dated three days later.

> I've been leaving clues everywhere I go, I'd make a hell of a suspect. I leave instructions at every hotel to forward my mail on to Paris. But I want to know now, I need to know.
>
> I want some kind of concrete reason why I should come home. I'm waiting for some word from you. I'll be at the Hotel Heliopolis in Athens on the 27th. Write to me.
>
> I love you...Absence makes the heart grow... farther away. That's what I think. Being so far away doesn't give me a sense of closeness, it just makes me feel incredibly distant. That's the way it ought to be.
>
> Tell me all the crazy things you're doing. I want to share them with you. Everywhere I go it's the same: the bonfires are burning and everyone's either a dancer or a martyr.
>
> Send me a picture of yourself, will you. No one believes that the man I tell them I'm in love with is a real person, not the taxi drivers, or the restaurant owners, or all the friends that I keep making and unmaking—they all think you're some kind of myth. Sorry, but that's the reaction I get here in the Old World whenever I say the words "Mexican detective."
>
> —ME

"That's all of them. Now what?" said the engineer, hanging up the telephone and crossing the last hotel off the list.

"Life goes on," Héctor said, drinking off half his soda in a single gulp. He was thirsty, and he felt like celebrating. "Thanks for the help, neighbor."

"Hey, any time, buddy, any time. I got a kick out of it."

"Are you going to be here all night?"

"Yeah, sure."

"Can you do me a favor? If someone calls and leaves a message for me, will you call radio station XEFS and give the message to El Cuervo Valdivia? Here, write down the phone numbers."

He handed him El Cuervo's card, then picked up the telephone and dialed a number.

"*Señora* Ferrer, please."

"Just a minute. Who's calling?"

"Belascoarán Shayne."

A brief silence before the actress's voice came on the line.

"Do you have any news about Elena?"

"We ought to find out pretty soon...I hope. If she comes home, can you call me at this number"—he gave her his office number—"and leave a message with Engineer Villareal? There's a chance she might be home around one in the morning."

"Are you sure?"

"No, I'm not sure. It's a long shot, but there's a chance it'll come through."

"I heard that you were over here the other night."

"I was just passing by..." he said, and hung up.

Next he called the radio station and asked El Cuervo to act as his liaison. El Cuervo liked the idea, and he agreed to transmit the cryptic message that Héctor dictated over the phone.

"Are you serious about blowing up a hotel, neighbor?" asked the engineer.

"Why do you ask?"

"Because I could get you a couple of sticks of dynamite, if you want it...I know where there's some blasting materials stashed at one of the jobs I work at. I could get you two or three sticks."

"Do you know how to use them?"

"Yep."

"It'd be great if you could get me a few, and show me how to use them."

"There's just one condition."

"Fine, whatever you want."

"You tell me what you want them for, and if I think it's okay, then you can have them."

"That seems fair enough. We'll talk about it later. Have fun."
Héctor hung his trench coat across his shoulders and went out.

A light rain had fallen, and the street smelled fresh and cool.
Héctor walked through the crowd of people getting out of the
last show at the Metropolitan Theater, got into his car, and drove
out toward Insurgentes and Engineer Camposanto's apartment.
When it came to stubbornness, he was becoming a real star.

He switched on the radio.

> *...this collection of Vietnamese poetry I was telling*
> *you about. There was one poem in particular, several*
> *lines, really, I was reading them and all of a sudden I*
> *felt like they'd been written specially for me. I brought*
> *it with me tonight. The poet's name is Luu Trong Lu,*
> *and he writes:*
> *"Do you talk on the radio? Do you work? We will*
> *always return to find each other in the thick of the*
> *struggle."*
> *Isn't that a beautiful idea?*
> *But enough of that for now. I've got something special*
> *for anybody out there that's too much in love, who's fallen*
> *too deep, everyone who's lovesick, and for all those lonely*
> *hearts out there as well. A dose of melodrama, to help*
> *you laugh at yourself just a little bit. This is a* bolero *by*
> *José Feliciano and Nosotros.*

It seemed as though Valdivia had gone to the bathroom but was
constipated, because the first song was followed by a second,
and then a third. At twenty to twelve, Héctor passed the traffic
circle at the Insurgentes Metro station. The smell of tacos and
barbecued meat almost turned him from his destination, but
he resisted the temptation.

> *And now, a personal message for some boys holed up*
> *in a certain hotel on Zaragoza Boulevard:*
> *You're in a very dangerous situation. You'd better*
> *hand over what you've got that doesn't belong to you.*

*It's not good to hold on to something against its will. If you don't give it up, you'll be paying a very high price.*

*Moving on, I'm happy to report that the wind tomorrow will be out of the east, and there are smooth conditions predicted for Xochimilco, Lago de Chapultepec, and Nuevo Lago.*

An African ritual melody surged through the car speakers.

A group of drunks were playing soccer in front of Camposanto's building and Héctor realized it was Saturday night. The engineer drove past Héctor just as he was about to park, taking him completely by surprise.

Camposanto had a full block on him by the time Héctor turned his car around, but he managed to keep up, maintaining the distance through a full set of *danzones*, a couple of blues tunes, and a ration of Swiss mountain songs played by request for the graveyard shift at a watch factory who called in to say they were falling asleep on the job. In between, El Cuervo put out a request for help in combating an infestation of rats in the Guerrero district, communicated the complaints of a group of neighbors against a Chiapan student whose wild parties disturbed the entire neighborhood, asked if there was someone who knew how to give injections and could help an elderly diabetic woman, read passages from Philip Agee's book on the CIA, and warned his listeners about the adulteration of ingredients at the Imperial Candy factory. Finally he came on with the message Héctor was waiting for:

*Here's a few personal messages for the folks out there: For Gustavo, from Lauro: The School of Sciences meeting for tomorrow has been canceled.*

*To my friend the detective: The woman in question says that Elena is home, safe and sound; they're waiting for you there.*

*For Maruja, from Julio Bañuelos: If you've moved out for good, at least come and take your junk away with you.*

>    And Alvarado says, "I have African stamps to trade
> for triangular stamps from any country. P.O. Box two
> thousand three hundred fifty-four, Postal Delegation
> number twenty..."

Composanto turned off Viaducto onto Zaragoza Boulevard, and Héctor chewed on the end of his last cigarette. Where the hell's he going now, he wondered. The engineer finally stopped in front of a cheap-looking hotel called Gemini 4, and Héctor waited for him to disappear inside the building before he got out and searched the block for the Rambler station wagon. He bought a pack of cigarettes in a late-night *taquería*, and returned to his car where he kept watch until six in the morning.

He was starting to develop a real grudge against this engineer who never seemed to sleep.

He followed him out toward Santa Clara in heavy morning traffic.

The city unleashed an army of humanity onto its streets. The city gave no quarter, made no allowances for lack of sleep, the encroaching cold, frigid limbs, bad moods, breakfasts caught on the run, acid indigestion, halitosis, upset stomach.

Every morning, in the same way, the city sent its soldiers out to do battle. She sent some out with power in their hands, and the rest with the everyday blessings of the street.

The city was a holy mess.

Once he was certain Camposanto was headed for the factory, Héctor stopped at a post office, and, leaning on the counter, wrote the letter he'd been carrying around in his head since the night before.

>    I'm waiting for you. Caught up in a triple mystery
> involving the murder of a gay engineer, a teenage girl
> with her arm in a cast, and a dead hero threatening
> to rise out of the grave.
>
>                                        —ME

He marked the envelope special delivery and covered it with stamps. At the last minute, he included a picture the upholsterer had taken with the janitor's Instamatic. The soles of his shoes filled the foreground, propped up on the edge of the old armchair, and behind them, the office in its usual state of chaos, crowned with a view of the coatrack where his thirty-eight hung in its shoulder holster alongside his wrinkled coat. He scribbled across the back of the photograph "A work of art," and inserted it in the envelope.

He drove on to the Delex plant, and left his car parked opposite the car he'd been following all night long.

He waited outside Rodríguez Cuesta's office for ten minutes, contemplating the virtues of the same secretary whose legs he'd been so taken with the last time. "Nice ass," he thought, and then tried to assume an objective and purely scientific attitude, by calculating the area of her buttocks in square inches. He was offered coffee and doughnuts, and listened to a joke about the former President of the Republic.

There was a rarefied atmosphere to Rodríguez Cuesta's office, and while the company president, after waving Héctor to a chair, sat signing papers, Belascoarán was overcome with a strange sensation. They were mortal, too, these captains of industry, he thought. They were mortal, too, and death could penetrate even the high walls that surrounded their middle-class existence. When all was said and done, there were limits to the impunity of the bourgeoisie.

"What's on your mind?" asked the Delex strongman, looking at Héctor.

"I want to know what it is exactly you want me to find out. I've been wanting to ask you since the other day."

"I wouldn't presume to second-guess you in your work, *Señor* Belascoarán," answered Rodríguez, smiling.

"I'll put it another way: What is Delex afraid of, other than its problems with the union?"

"I'm not sure what you want to know. Or maybe I just don't want to answer the question…I'm sure you're not interested in our analysis of the current economic situation."

"Not in the least," said Héctor, standing up.

"I hope you'll have the good sense to maintain a purely professional attitude regarding our adversaries in the union."

"I'd like to collect that advance we were talking about the other day." Héctor ignored the president's comment.

"You'll have to talk with Guzmán Vera."

Héctor left the factory with a check for fifteen thousand pesos in his pocket, and the feeling that he was walking away from a mountain of unanswered questions. The morning mist wrapped itself tenderly around him, ignoring the nervous tics that rippled around his bloodshot eyes with a variety and an intensity previously unknown.

# Chapter Seven

"Do you believe in love at first sight?" asked the girl. "I believe in confusion," said Paul Newman.

"Hi," said Belascoarán from the doorway.

The girl smiled from where she lay in the bed under the blue comforter.

"What'd you do to scare them like that?"

Héctor shrugged his shoulders.

"They sure were surprised. They kept asking me who you were, who's that son of a bitch who shot at us the other day, who kicked me in the jaw...I just told them you were my guardian angel, and they only got more pissed off."

"Did they hurt you?"

"They hit me a couple of times when they kidnapped me. It wasn't bad. After that they were just trying to scare me... Threatening to rape me, lock me in a room with a rabid dog, burn the soles of my feet...Just a lot of talk."

She looked extremely fragile, with her arm in its cast resting on the comforter, her hair falling across her face, a Margarita Gauthier smile. The soft morning light filtered through the blue curtains and fell at the foot of the bed.

"Sit down," she said.

Héctor sat on the rug, stretched, and then lay down. He pulled a cigarette from his pocket and set fire to it. The girl handed him an ashtray.

"Are you okay?"

"Just tired."

"Were you really going to blow up the hotel?"

Héctor nodded.

"They sure were scared all right. They're not professionals, you know."

"What are the professionals like?"

"Oh, I don't know. More efficient, I suppose. Meaner. Those guys didn't believe what they were saying."

Héctor smoked quietly, watching the columns of smoke rise toward the ceiling. He could have lain there for hours, watching the rising smoke, resting, letting the soft morning sink into his veins, maybe have drunk a cup of coffee or a soda pop.

"Are you going to tell me what's going on?" he asked suddenly.

"Not yet."

"What do you think about going to take a little vacation where those guys can't find you?"

She said she'd like it.

"Come on, then."

The girl jumped out of bed.

"Can I go like this or should I change first?"

"It's up to you."

"Close your eyes."

Héctor did as he was told. Luxuriating in the softness of the rug, he started to drift off to sleep. There was the sound of drawers being opened and closed, the rustle of cloth against skin.

"Okay, I'm ready. Isn't Mama going to be angry?"

"Let her," said the detective, as he lifted himself slowly from the floor.

The pressure was off for the moment in the race to find the fifty-thousand-peso-whatever-it-was, and with the added certainty that Elena was safe in his sister's hands, Héctor was able to turn his attention back to the search for Emiliano Zapata.

Using a geologic map of the state of Morelos he tried to isolate the areas where caves were most likely to be found. He began by ruling out the zones where Zapata had enjoyed his strongest influence. If Zapata were there, the people would have found him on their own, and wouldn't have needed Héctor's help. If Zapata's cave existed at all, it would have to be somewhere outside his traditional stomping grounds. So far so good. It soon became clear, however, that while certain rocky formations were more promising than others, caves could be found in practically any geographic area whatsoever, with the obvious exception of the open plains. After four hours of careful study he realized he was getting nowhere fast. So he went on to consider the possibility that the same Emiliano Zapata that had cast his lot with the Sandinistas in Nicaragua would have gone on to participate in the 1932 uprising in El Salvador, and later gone to fight with the International Brigades in Spain. Héctor scanned books and photographs, and read through lists of names, but there was no record of any fifty-seven-year-old man who even remotely matched Zapata's description among the brave Mexicans who had gone off to fight in the Spanish Civil War.

He felt like a member of an esoteric sect dedicated to the preservation of ghosts. Maybe that was the problem: he was going at the whole thing more like a historian or a journalist than a detective. He decided to lay aside any preconceptions and simply focus his energies on tracking down a man named Emiliano Zapata, as if millions of words had never been written about him, streets baptized with his name, or statues dedicated to his memory. The Zapata he was looking for was now a ninety-seven-year-old man who had disappeared back in 1916. It was Héctor's job to find him, sixty years later.

How did people get to Mexico from Central America in the 1930s?

By boat, of course. Through Veracruz or Acapulco. And a man like Zapata, trying to conceal his true identity, would probably have chosen Veracruz, as the port farthest from his native Morelos. At the office of the Navy, Héctor asked to see the records from the port of Veracruz for the years 1934 and '35. They laughed in his face.

There was always the possibility, if he wanted to stick to the story of the old man in the *cantina*, of exploring a connection with the *campesino* leader Rubén Jaramillo.

Héctor reread Jaramillo's excellent autobiography, but came up with nothing. Not the slighest hint of any kind of relationship with a still-living Zapata, which certainly would have had a tremendous impact on Jaramillo, who was Zapata's ideological heir. Of course, the connection might have occurred during one of the periods not covered in the book. Possibly during one of the less eventful periods of his life, such as when Jaramillo worked as the director of the market in Santa Julia, or, on the other hand, during the tumultuous period of the second uprising, which lasted until Jaramillo's murder. Another couple of ideas occurred to him. He jotted them down on a small piece of paper which he stuffed into his pocket, and then, like a man putting on a different jacket, he crossed over into another story.

There was a question he wanted to ask Marisa Ferrer: Where did she get the smack? But just then the afternoon headlines caught his eye, and he had to change stories again: UNION AGITATORS ARRESTED IN ENGINEER'S MURDER.

War had broken out at Delex.

> The accused murderers were taken into custody today as they were leaving the Delex factory. Arrested were: Gustavo Fuentes, Leonardo Ibáñez, and Jesús Contreras. The police action was carried out by Commander Paniagua, head of the Sixth Squadron of the Judicial Police for the State of Mexico. The police were met with resistance from the accused's co-workers, who tried to prevent the arrests from taking place. However, the men were finally removed from the factory and handed over to agents of the public prosecutor...

The article continued with a description of the murder.

Héctor drove to his office and found the list of possible suspects that Delex had originally supplied him. It turned out that two of the accused men weren't even on the company's own list, meaning either that they hadn't been at the factory that day, or that they worked a different shift from the one during which the crime was committed. That's how crude the frame-up was.

He phoned Delex and asked to speak with Rodríguez Cuesta.

"It's obviously ridiculous, *Señor* Belascoarán," Rodríguez began. "But Commander Paniagua insisted. Certainly you understand…By all means, I want you to continue with your investigation…Although Paniagua's likely to give you trouble if you get in his way…One last thing. From now on, I want you to deliver your reports to me personally. There should be no extra copies made, not even for your own files. I will be the only one with access to the information, and you and I alone will decide how to proceed."

What had he meant when he said Paniagua was likely to give him trouble?

Try as he might, he couldn't stop the gears from turning. A sudden, massive headache forced Belascoarán to squeeze his eyes shut. It was time to get some sleep. Things would clear up as time went by, and if they went according to the jumbled plans slowly taking shape in his head, he was going to have a long night ahead of him.

As he was leaving, the telephone rang.

"She ran out on me. I went up to the counter to pay the bill, and when I came back…"

"Don't worry about it, Elisa. It's not your fault."

He left his car parked in front of the office and rode the subway home instead.

His head throbbed stubbornly with pain as he walked slowly up to the door of his apartment and fit the key into the lock. He headed straight for the bathroom, opened up both taps, and pushed his head under the running water. Dropping his coat on the floor, he unbuttoned his shirt, pushed his hand through his hair, and staggered in the direction of his bed. He was surprised to find it already occupied.

"When I saw you this morning I had the idea you'd be going to bed before too long," said the girl with her arm in a cast, hiding under the sheets in the soft shadows.

The room was in its customary state of disarray: clothes on the floor, books, newspapers lying here and there, dirty dishes, half-empty glasses tucked into the most unlikely places. Héctor took in the disaster zone, thinking that no matter how much he cleaned up, it always looked the same. As a matter of fact, it was just the other day that he'd gone through and picked up a few things. At least he'd washed the ashtrays and the room didn't smell like stale cigarettes.

"I usually sleep at the office when…" he started to say, but stopped himself. What the hell was he doing giving explanations no one had asked for?

"I hope you don't mind my coming over here like this."

"I…" he said, and stopped again.

He lit a cigarette.

"Do you believe in love at first sight?" asked the girl.

"I believe in confusion," he answered, quoting Paul Newman, from a movie he'd seen on television a couple of months back.

"Who is she?" asked the girl, pointing to a picture of the woman with the ponytail, taken a year earlier as she followed him along San Juan de Letrán.

"A woman."

"I could tell…Just a woman…that's all?"

"A woman I'm in love with, or something like that," he said, feeling defeated.

Possibility #1: I go to bed with her and to hell with the rest. If this damn headache gets worse, it'll be the least I deserve.

Possibility #2: I interrogate her until I find out what the hell's going on and what she's hiding that's worth fifty thousand pesos.

Possibility #3: I get a blanket and sleep on the floor.

He chose number three.

Elena watched him unhappily. Slowly, she got up from the bed.

She had pretty legs, and small, pointed breasts. The arm in its cast gave her a boyish appearance that was immediately dispelled by the lovely "V" of her loins. Her hair fell to one side of her face.

"Don't you like me?"

"Look, it's not that simple…I'll tell you what, why don't you just slide over and give me half of the bed, and let me go to sleep. When I wake up I'll try to explain it to you."

She did as she was told.

And in part because it takes a lot of effort to ignore a bedful of woman, in part because it wasn't for nothing he'd spent so many months in the clutches of loneliness and celibacy, and a little bit because his fatigue nudged him toward those open arms…and a lot because he was attracted to the girl's warmth and vitality. For all these things, and others that he'd never be able to put into words, six hours later Héctor found himself making love. He was careful not to bump into the broken arm in its cast.

"I always thought that guardian angels were sexless."

"I always thought that Catholic school girls kept their virginity locked in a little box."

"Sure, but when the box is at the pawnshop, what's it matter? That's the whole secret. In Sister María's class, she's probably the only virgin there, and that's because she's a lesbian."

Héctor's headache was almost gone, leaving him with only the slightest feeling of discomfort.

The room was completely dark. Héctor tried to guess the time, but the days and nights all blended together in his mind, and the brief hours of sleep he'd managed to steal over the past week seemed like mere accidents, momentary interruptions in an otherwise endless succession of events.

He dressed in full view of the girl, to make it clear he regretted nothing. His clothes were scattered on the floor around the bed, where they'd been thrown in the heat of battle.

"Can you get back to my sister's house from here on your own?"

"Can't I stay here?"

"Look, the only reason you left your own house to begin with was to go someplace safe. You're not safe here."

She got out of the bed reluctantly, and got dressed, moving her injured arm with some difficulty. She asked Héctor to help her button up her shirt.

He caressed her cheek, and she kissed his hand.

"I'm ready to tell you the story…"

"We'll have breakfast tomorrow at Elisa's. You can tell me then."

"I'll be waiting for you."

Her words hung in the air as Héctor stood at the window and watched her head down the street. When he saw her turn toward Insurgentes, he went out. He had an appointment to keep with someone who wasn't waiting for him.

"Tell me, Camposanto, what's Rodríguez Cuesta afraid of?"

He felt as though he'd stumbled into a life-size dollhouse by mistake, in a mistaken dream he couldn't find his way out of. There was a place for everything and everything was set meticulously, obsessively in its place. A Siamese cat strolled across the floor.

Camposanto, wrapped in a gray robe and holding a glass of cognac in his hand, was starting to show signs of discomfort. Up until that point, their conversation had traveled the route of the standard courtesies, like the small train chugging around the zoo in Chapultepec park.

"Why ask me? Why not talk to Haro, or Guzmán Vera?"

"Because you're a homosexual, just like Alvarez Cerruli was, just like Bravo Osorio, the other engineer murdered two months earlier at another factory in Santa Clara. Now don't get me wrong, Engineer, I don't mean any offense…Or am I mistaken?"

Camposanto bit his lip at the sound of the word *homosexual*. Then he turned to stare angrily at he detective. "So I'm gay. What's it to you?" he demanded.

"My guess is there's some kind of connection there…But that's not what I wanted to know about just yet. What I came to find out is what your boss is afraid of."

"You really think he's afraid of something?"

"I want an answer, not another question."

"He's probably afraid there'd be a scandal."

"No, that's not it. He wouldn't need me for that. The cops are perfectly capable of tying the whole thing up neatly enough. He needs me for something the cops can't do for him, to find out

who the real murderer is. That's who he's afraid of, the real mur-
derer. Rodríguez already knows who it is, but he wants proof."
Surprise showed in Camposanto's eyes. Héctor had his answer.
"Thanks for your help, Engineer." Héctor got to his feet.

He went back to the beginning, to the place of questions and
answers, to the place where the whole thing started from, with
the three separate bundles of paper. Now at least one of the
mysteries was starting to take some shape.

He went back to stare at the three photos tacked up on the
wall, the point of departure for his quest. He'd carried up a case
of soda pop, stashing it in the office "safe," and had been sitting
at his desk for half an hour, writing notes. Now he flipped back
through his notebook and thought:

> The president of a large corporation, who has interests
> in an unknown number of other companies, and a
> great deal of financial power besides (find out how
> many, which ones, and how much), hires a detective
> to find the murderer of a homosexual engineer (the
> second in two months).
>
> Publicly, what he wants to do is frame the union for
> the murder.
>
> But he also wants the evidence against the real mur-
> derer for himself.
>
> Assumption: He knows who the murderer is, and
> he's afraid of him.
>
> What does he need the proof for? Simple curiosity?
> No, curiosity isn't worth the cost of the investigation,
> or letting someone else in on the information.
>
> He wants the evidence in order to put some kind of
> pressure on the guilty party. This seems to indicate

that he already has some connection with the murderer.

One question leads to the other…Who is it, and why should Rodríguez Cuesta be afraid of him?

Why kill a pair of homosexual engineers? Are the two murders really connected?

Why would X want to kill a homosexual engineer?

Is X also a homosexual? Were they involved in some kind of trouble together?

Is Alvarez Cerruli the link between X and Rodríguez Cuesta, or vice versa? Or is that a two-way street?

What other connections are there between X and R.C.?

Guilt by association, blackmail?

The thing to do is find X.

Jesus, what a mess. He crossed out X and wrote WW in its place. That made it sound even more exotic.

All the same, there was an appealing coherence to the whole thing.

"Care for some coffee, neighbor?" asked the sewer expert, buried once again in his maps, with their strange cabalistic symbols.

"No thanks. I think I'll have a soda instead."

"I brought you what we talked about…It's in the 'safe.'"

Héctor inspected the three sticks of dynamite. They had short braided fuses made from a reddish string.

"They've got twenty-second fuses. You can light them with a cigarette. If you bury them, or cover them with some heavy material, they'll do more damage. If they're detonated in an open space, they'll kill anything within a radius of about eight yards. I'd treat them with respect if I were you. They might surprise you."

Héctor nodded. He looked at the dynamite with enormous respect.

◇◇◇

"This is it," said Elisa, as she untied the cord around the shoe box.

They sat together in an old oak-paneled booth in the back of a restaurant.

"Wait a second, Elisa."

"What is it?"

"I was just thinking the old man's got something bizarre in store for us, and I don't know where I'm going to find the time to deal with anything else right now," said Héctor.

"It won't hurt just to find out what he wants," said Carlos.

Elisa pulled off the last of the string and opened the box. Inside there was a gray notebook with two rubber bands around it, a nautical map folded sixteen times, and a small folder. At the bottom, a blank envelope. Elisa took each item out of the box and set them in a row on the table.

"I suppose we ought to start with the letter."

# Chapter Eight

## A Notebook, a Map, a Folder, and a Letter

And he thought that he should be one of these men, one of these who work outside in the sun, not those who seek pleasure in the shade.

—Pio Baroja

"No, try the notebook first," said Carlos.

Elisa pulled off the rubber bands and opened the cover.

My story is a story of struggle, a product of the times I lived in. Were it up to me, I would have preferred not to have stained my hands with the blood of other men.

But it couldn't have been otherwise. I have killed with my own hands for an ideal. And the ideal only got further from my reach.

I became a socialist when I was thirteen, and I suppose I'm still a socialist today. I came to socialism through the hunger of my people, and my own desire for justice. I worked as a fireman on a small ship, carrying pharmaceuticals to various ports on the Cantabrian coast, at a time when it was easier to ship goods by boat than by train in the north of Spain. We were never averse to taking on other jobs, and frequently we worked as smugglers or fishermen. I'm still very proud to have been, at the age of fourteen, one of the founders of the Seaman's Union of San Sebastián, bringing together more than a thousand longshoremen, sailors, fishermen, and dockers in the Basque region.

I had a reputation for being stubborn and headstrong, and I'm sure I earned it. But I was also known as a man of my word.

My youthful brashness often got me into trouble, and there were many times when I wasn't able to get work and had to return home empty-handed. We lived very humbly, since my father's starvation wages as a municipal employee were never enough to make ends meet or improve our family's desperate situation.

We went hungry often enough.

This all happened a long time ago, and for that reason I never told you about it before. In the same way, I've never talked much about the other things I've done in my life. I always believed that each of you had your own life to live, and that an old man's stories would get in the way more than they would help.

The revolution broke out in October 1934. At that time I was in the beautiful Asturian port of Aviles, in command of a worm-eaten sailboat. We were smuggling arms under orders from the Socialist Party, which was preparing itself to fight against the fascist attempt to take power. As a result of my small contribution to the events of that period, and our subsequent defeat, I was compelled to spend more than a year working out of the south of Spain as a sailor on ships bound for Morocco. I took a false name, and was completely cut off from my family, who thought I'd escaped to France. After a while I renewed my contacts with the party, and collaborated in writing and distributing *The Southern Seaman*. We reorganized the cadre of the long-shore union, and helped comrades escaping to Africa. During this time I came to know the Moroccan and Tunisian coastline like the back of my hand, or perhaps better, if that's possible, as well as the untamed coast around Spanish Sahara, Guinea, and Sidi Ifni. I made many good friends, and I found out that the white man's world isn't the only one there is. It was an amazing revelation for a twenty-five-year-old Basque. I'll tell you, I would have liked to have been born Basque-African. My Basque heritage is something I'll never turn my back on, ever. It's something I'll always be proud of. During those hard times, in the port of Tunis, I knew my first woman, and I became a man.

I loved the sea as few have ever loved her, but I loved the struggle even more.

With the amnesty, I went home to San Sebastián and participated in the reorganization of the unions there. But the fascist uprising took me by surprise while I was nursing my sick father in a mountain village. My father died two days later, but I couldn't be with him. I had already gone to enlist, and asked to be assigned to the front lines. I served as a militia captain with a brave company of hard-fighting socialists and anarcho-syndicalists. When the Northern Front fell, I took charge of the evacuation of many comrades, slipping them through the blockade by boat, and safely on into France. I then crossed back over the border and was assigned the task of supplying the rest of our troops by sea.

Constantly outwitting the fascist ships, as well as the German and Italian, we kept Loyal Spain in supplies and ammunition.

I'm proud to say that during those two years I never took a day's rest, nor did I want one. There were many who acted otherwise. But this is not a time to point fingers. There were many who did their duty the same as me. And there were many more who died. Their blood is still on our hands, a debt unpaid.

The war ended with our defeat, and I sailed out of Valencia on a fishing boat called the *María Engracia*, which we had fit with two English motors powerful enough to run an armored gunboat. There were seventeen of us lucky enough to escape together, and out in the middle of the Mediterranean, along the African coast, we swore never to forgive, never to forget, and always to continue the struggle.

With the war over, our comrades in Africa were put into concentration camps by the French, who wished to avoid any problems, and wishing to avoid them, ended up with more than their share.

With the help of some old friends we changed our ship's registration to a port in Costa Rica, and received false documents through a network operated by the Communist Party out of Casablanca. The operation was run by a much loved pair of comrades, German Jews, who knew more about the art of forgery than María Castaña Castaña herself.

In the months following the end of the war in Spain, and before the beginning of the Second World War, we spent our time improving the condition of our ship, smuggling cigarettes through the French ports just to have something to eat, running freight along the coasts as far north as Albania, and stockpiling arms and ammunition. Two of our comrades left us during this time, hoping to reunite themselves with their families.

When I left Valencia, I left behind a tremendous love for the woman who is now your mother. We met while she was singing for the International Brigades, and we spent several days together, discovering love in the midst of the hurricane of war. I told her I would go to her country and find her again some day when I was free to do so. As you already know, she was Irish, from a good family. Her father was a scholar of ancient letters who was proud that his youngest daughter chose to go perform for the fighting men of Spain.

I wrote to her every chance I could, throughout the course of the long war that followed, keeping our love alive.

We were pirates. We attacked Italian freighters both in port and on the open sea. Once we even sank a German Coast Guard vessel off the coast of Tripoli.

We had no flag, and time and again we changed the name and the appearance of our ship. We were lone wolves. Two of our good comrades fell in these early battles, Mariano Helguera and Vicente Díaz Robles, both anarcho-syndicalists from Cádiz. Another, Valeriano Corral, was wounded very badly and we were forced to bring him ashore. We left him behind and never heard of him again. He was Catalan, belonging to no party, but as good as gold, and more dedicated to the struggle than anyone.

The English wanted to make use of our experience, and we cooperated with them. Within the framework of that struggle, there was no room for petty differences. We smuggled arms to the Yugoslav partisans, and carried Canadian commandos to missions in Northern Africa, and later on, to the coast of France.

Two boats eventually made up our pirate armada. The first was nicknamed *El Loco*, and we called the second *The Dawn of the People*, although it was officially called *The Bearded Fish*, written in Arabic on the hull and registered in Liberia. On ship we lived in absolute democracy and freedom, and although I acted as captain, it was by the open agreement of my comrades. As a group, we decided to carry out several actions against Spanish ports in the hands of Franco's soldiers. We attacked an armed customs post on the Baleares Islands, and later sank two small fascist gunboats in the port of Alicante.

In spite of the diversity of our actions, and our connections with the many different antifascist groups in North Africa, we felt very strongly drawn to the struggle of the French Resistance, where many of our countrymen were fighting as well. We worked particularly closely with a Greek named Tsarakis, whose *nom de guerre* was Christian. Together we participated in a successful attack on the German naval command in Marseilles, and in the transport of arms to the French Resistance. In this period we lost three more of our comrades. I will tell you their names to keep their memory alive: Valentín Suárez, a socialist mechanic from Burgos; Leoncio Pradera Villa, a communist from Leon, a wonderfully warm-hearted man and a loyal friend; and a one-eyed fellow named Beltrán, a unionist from Andalucia.

In 1944, near the Albanian coast, we encountered an Italian gunboat. They thought we were carrying fresh fruit, and tried to board our ship with the intention of commandeering our cargo. We fought for twenty minutes, our boats lashed together, until not one of them was left alive.

Inside we found 23 kilos of gold coins from different countries, bound for Italy under the orders of Marshal D' Ambrosio. We took the treasure and hid it on the north coast of Africa, with the idea of using it after the victory in Europe to finance the liberation of Spain. We fervently believed at that time that no one would deny us aid once the fascists were driven out of Europe.

In 1945 I put ashore in France and joined a battalion formed almost entirely of Spaniards, which went on to fight at the head of the Leclerc division. Disembarking with me were Simón Matías, who was killed in a German counter-attack in Czechoslovakia, and Gervasio Cifuentes, from Mieres, a very close friend who died without family a few years ago here in Mexico.

Six of our comrades stayed aboard *El Loco*, helping the English sweep for mines in the sea around Malta.

When the war ended we found out they had been killed, gone down with our beloved ship in the middle of the Mediterranean. Somehow, my destiny brought me to Mexico. I had married your mother, and after so many years of blood and war I only wanted to rest. I was discouraged by the defeat in Spain and the treachery of the Allies, and I ended up like so many others: dropping anchor in a friendly port, and turning my exile into a period of waiting without end.

Cifuentes and I often spoke of the twenty-three kilos of gold coins. He worked as an accountant in a shoe factory, I got a job in a publishing house, in which I still work today as assistant manager.

That's my story. Now you are grown-up. I don't want to set an example, since there's no better example than the one you set for yourselves. I just wanted to leave you with a handful of stories so that you won't say your father was always a peaceful old man who spent his evenings reading in the garden in the house in Coyoacán. I wasn't always old. It's just that time passes."

"What do you do with a story like that?" Héctor asked himself. "How do you fit it into your life, how do you connect the past with the present?" The papers in the folder were clippings from French, English, Italian, and German newspapers, interviews and articles, confirming bits and pieces of the old man's story. There was even a pair of documents issued by the French Army, testifying to the activities of *El Loco* in support of the Resistance, and conferring upon Captain Belascoarán and his crew the Medal of the Resistance.

The map covered a highly magnified portion of the North African coast, showing the location of the buried treasure.

"So now what?" asked Elisa. "Are we supposed to go to Africa and dig for buried treasure?"

"I'm going to go out of my mind," said Héctor.

"It all sounds kind of like an adventure story, but I guess if Papa wanted us to go find the gold, then I'm willing to do it," said Carlos.

"Open up the letter, Elisa."

She tore open the envelope and removed a single piece of paper.

> My dear children, it is my desire that, since my good friend and comrade Cifuentes died without any descendents, you three should fulfill our last wish. Read the notebook I've included with this letter and go find the gold. After paying for your costs, give the rest of it to the Spanish labor unions fighting openly against the regime in the name of the working people.
>
> I know that I can trust you to pay this debt for me.
>
> —JMBA

"How about a soda pop?" asked Héctor.

"Coffee for me," said Elisa.

"The old man's got a point: it's the right thing to do. It's just that the last thing I need right now is to start dreaming about the coast of North Africa," said Héctor.

"Don't worry, Brother, we don't have to leave tomorrow."

"Well, why not?" asked Héctor, smiling.

# Chapter Nine

It was a vast thicket of sinuous and winding paths called labyrinth.

—R. Ocken

Inaccessible to the light, with infinite detours and a thousand treacherous, confusing, and tortuous paths; it was impossible to enter into it and find the way back.

—M. Meunier

He had a name now, which was more than he'd had before, plus the hope that the old man hadn't changed it at some point in the intervening years. Isaías Valdez. Entering the market, Belascoarán wandered from stall to stall, guided by a magic hand that pointed the way: "Go talk to *don* Manuel, he was around in those days…" "They say that *doña* Chole's been here since they opened the market. And *don* Manuel, he knew Rubén Jaramillo." He wandered from vegetable stalls to butcher's stalls, spoke with aged fruit sellers, and the owner of a chicken shop, but without result. After a while he changed his tack, and stopped trying to salvage the name Isaías Valdez from the mists of people's memories.

"A buddy of Jaramillo's? He had plenty, let me tell you. They used to come in from the country all the time, he'd bring them in, and give them some fruit or some bread, and show them around the market while they talked…What's that? Somebody from the market, from right here?…Let me see, there was a lot of them…in his late sixties, huh?…sixty-seven…Oh, you must mean *don* Eulalio Zaldívar. Sure, that's it, he and Jaramillo were real tight. He didn't talk much, though…Let me see if I've got a picture of the vendors from back then. Here we go, this here's Jaramillo, and over here on the right side, you almost can't see him, that's *don* Eulalio—he always wore a hat, and a bandana around his neck, like he was sick. He had a real hoarse voice. Sold fruit, in that stall over there…He went away in 'forty-seven, but then he came back. Only, he went away again about six years ago. He was terribly old by then, poor guy, didn't have any family either. An address? No, he didn't leave an address…"

A shadow, a ghost, a grayish blur in the background of an old photograph. Could that really be Zapata, reduced to a gray blur, while his life was rewritten in government textbooks, and on commemorative plaques.

The fairy tale of *don* Emiliano. Where to look next?

"So let's have it, what's the story?"

The girl eyed him blankly. It was the old family house in Coyoacán, where Elisa was living for the time being. They sat together in a shady corner of the garden, sipping an *agua de chía* prepared by the maid. Héctor hung his coat in the branches of a tree, and rolled up his shirtsleeves. The butt of his .38 protruded obscenely from its shoulder holster like a bird of ill omen.

It was a stain under his armpit that no antiperspirant could remove. He hung the gun and holster from another branch.

"I can't tell you, not now."

The girl walked over and put the tree between herself and Héctor. The detective watched her through the lower branches. She circled her good arm around the trunk and held on.

"You never tried to kill yourself, did you?"

"Never."

Héctor collected his jacket, and the gun in its holster. He would have preferred the sunny courtyard, full of dazzling reflections, a cold glass of lemonade, a good cigar, a novel by Salagari. It could have been a good afternoon. He would have preferred…

"I'm all ears," said the company president in the artificial hush and semidarkness of his office, infringed upon only by the bright rays of sunlight filtering through the edges of the venetian blinds, and the distant hum of the factory.

The air at the plant was full of tension. Groups of scabs lurked around the front gate, and shotgun-toting security guards patrolled the grounds. As he passed by one of the bays, Héctor noticed there was work stoppage in progress. The workers stood motionless in front of their machines, as if observing a moment of silence for a fallen comrade. Foremen ran from one man to the next, threatening, intimidating. The work stoppage only took effect in one section at a time, so that while one group of men lay down their tools, the others kept working. After exactly five minutes, the group Héctor was watching went back to work and the forklift operators shut down.

He overheard a discussion between an engineer and a lift-truck operator: "Get this heap moving, you idiot." "You get it moving." "You're getting paid to drive this thing, not me. What the hell do you think you're doing?" "Haven't you noticed there's a work stoppage going on, you idiot?"

The president's office was a backwater separated from the boiling current, like a stage set belonging to a different play, another story, or a different scene in the same TV drama.

"I've come to ask you a few questions."

"Fire away," answered the president, removing a pack of Philip Morris from his vest pocket.

Where else had Héctor seen the same brand? On the table next to the fat man's bed…

"What are you afraid of? What is it about the guy you have me looking for that's got you so rattled? How come you don't just tell me who it is? What's his name?"

The other man glanced at him momentarily, his eyes hidden behind a cloud of smoke.

"I'm paying you to find the answers."

"Is that what you want, the answers to these questions?"

"I want the murderer's name, and the proof that he did it." Héctor stood up.

"I don't like you, Belascoarán," said the president.

"The feeling's mutual," said Héctor, and he threw his half-smoked cigarette onto the rug, and walked out the door. He didn't look back.

◇◇◇

"Make yourself comfy, neighbor," said Gilberto the plumber, wheeling the swivel chair out into the room, while Carlos the upholsterer dusted it with a rag.

"Care for a soft drink?"

"What's going on? Did I win the lottery or something?"

"Lottery?"

"One soda coming up."

"Someone called to leave a couple of messages and since…"

"Go on and tell him," urged Carlos, handing Héctor a tamarind-flavored soda pop.

"They said you're dead meat. They said they're going to kill you."

"Who says?"

"On the telephone."

"How many times did they call?"

"Twice."

"Oh, well, if it's just twice," Héctor said, and took a big swig from the soda.

"There was something else…" The plumber picked up the newspaper where he'd written the message and read, "'Did it ever occur to you that police commanders can be faggots, too?'"

"What?"

"If it ever occurred to you that police commanders could be faggots, too."

"Who wants to know?"

"How am I supposed to know? The guy calls up and asks if you're here and I say no, that you're probably out farting around somewhere like you always are…"

"That's the pot calling the kettle black," interjected the upholsterer.

"…but since your secretary and I just happened to be in the office, that if he wanted to leave you a message, and the guy says to me to tell you this thing about if it ever occurred to you that…"

Héctor glanced around until he found the newspaper from two days before sitting on top of the armchair:

> …The police action was carried out by Comandante Paniagua, head of the Sixth Squadron of the Judicial Police for the State of Mexico…

The link between Alvarez Cerruli and the company president, the link of fear, could just possibly be a commander of the Judicial Police…Was that the answer?

In Alameda Park, in front of Bellas Artes, a man was swallowing gasoline and spitting fire. The city was overrun by Indian women selling nuts. The newspapers announced the resignation of the governor of Oaxaca.

Belascoarán drained his *café con leche*, and stepped out of the little restaurant. A few seconds earlier, the man he was following had carefully placed his tip on the table and stood up to go.

He was a heavyset man, big without being fat, dressed in a light-colored suit with a bright blue tie. His hair was very black and he wore a pair of dark glasses over a bulbous nose. Belascoarán imagined the revolver strapped to his hip, the revolver that compelled him to keep his jacket buttoned down low, and to spread a little Nivea on his left thigh every now and then where the muzzle rubbed uncomfortably. The gun at his belt, a habit that came from watching too many TV westerns, and a throwback to his days as a small-time, small-town gunman flashing his second member where everyone could see it.

Offering a hundred pesos here, a hundred pesos there, making the rounds of the small cafes in Bucareli where the news hounds hung out, Belascoarán had put together a sketchy but intriguing portrait of the man he was following:

He was born in Puebla, but grew up in Los Altos de Jalisco. Twice he had stood trial for murder, cooling his heels miserably in a Guadalajara jail. And even though he was found innocent, his hands and his gun were forever stained with blood. Later on, he worked as a hired gun for the mayor of Atotonilco, commander of the Judicial Police in Lagos de Moreno. In 1952 he became deputy chief of the Judicial Police in Coahuila, participating actively in the repression of the miners of Nueva Rosita. In 1960 he went into business as the owner of an ice factory in Guanajuato. In '68 he reappeared as a member of the Judicial Police in the State of Mexico, where he climbed the ladder rapidly. Three years ago he was promoted to commander.

The man walked with a slow step, in the way of an old buzzard stalking a partner in the village dance. Passing out from under the shadow of the Latin America Tower, he turned onto Calle Madero, stopping twice, once in front of a men's clothing store to admire a vest in the window, and later at a camera shop where he gazed attentively at a pair of binoculars.

He had a reputation as a closemouthed man with an iron fist. The word on the street was that he was involved in breaking the strikes in Naucalpan in '75, and that he had personally beaten jailed students from the School of Sciences and Humanities. The rest of his activities were cloaked in silence.

When the man stopped for a third time to gaze into a store window, Héctor started to wonder if he wasn't aware he was being followed. The detective halted in front of the Americana Bookstore, and peeled off his trench coat.

A pair of strange characters stepped past him at this predetermined signal. One of them was crowned with a Sherwin Williams painter's cap, and the other, a bearded man, carried an upholsterer's fabric sampler under his arm.

"...Of course he's going to pay us overtime. What else can he do? Otherwise we can drop the chase whenever we want..." Héctor overheard Gilberto saying as they passed by.

He smiled, then waited a couple of minutes before stepping back into the street. The big man with the dark glasses was out of sight, and Héctor's two accomplices were just turning left at the corner of Isabel la Católica. Elisa waited on her motorcycle at the curb.

"Coming for a ride?"

"Sure, let's go. Be sure to keep your distance."

"Where's your car?"

"I left it off at Juárez when he stopped at that cafe."

Time was running out, and he was starting to hate the city for the twelve-million-headed monster it was. Night invaded the office through the window. If sleeplessness and fatigue were the symbols for the first half of the story, now the labyrinth dominated the scene. And a labyrinth, by definition, contains a way out, but that was the hardest thing of all about the impasse the three mysteries had each run into. There was a way out, he knew it, he could almost feel it, almost smell it…And yet he could just as easily walk right past it and never know.

Héctor pasted a piece of paper under Zapata's picture, picked up a pen, and wrote:

> 1924: Tampico.
> 1926: in Nicaragua with Sandino—Captain Zenón Enríquez.
> 1934: issued passport in Costa Rica.
> 1944: works in the Dos de Abril Market, until '47.
> Eulalio Zaldívar. Returns from '62 until '66.
> Lives in Olivar de los Padres as Isaías Valdez.
> ??

He thought for a second and crossed out the question marks. It was better just to leave it blank. He stuck a second piece of paper under the picture of the dead engineer. This time he wrote:

> Alvarez Cerruli. Murdered. Homosexual.
>
> The company president: Rodríguez Cuesta. Afraid of something. Blackmail?
>
> A previous murder: also a homosexual.
>
> A cop.
>
> Classically speaking: show opportunity, motive, and method. Commander Paniagua.

"What're you writing over there, neighbor?" asked the nocturnal sewer expert at Héctor's back.

"Maybe you can help me, Engineer. You're used to moving in these circles…"

"Sometimes it feels like I spend all my time running around in circles, but…"

"No, I mean industrial circles."

"You and me both, neighbor."

"What sort of smuggling operation could an upstanding industrialist get himself involved in that might open him up to blackmail?"

"Like what kind of industrialist?"

"Like the President of Delex Steel."

Without knowing more about Rodríguez Cuesta, there was no way to find the connection between the source of the blackmail and the person doing the blackmailing, much less the link with the two murdered engineers.

What Rodríguez Cuesta wanted was the final link in the chain: Judicial Police Commander Paniagua. Wasn't it Rodríguez Cuesta, after all, who had made the call putting Héctor onto Paniagua's trail?

But Rodríguez Cuesta was after the whole chain, not just the individual links. If Héctor wanted to cut a deal on behalf of the independent union, he was going to need a bargaining chip. He added to his list:

The world of a company president. Smuggling?

Other possibilities? Women, drugs, is R.C. a
homosexual, too?

Suddenly it occurred to him that he didn't know a damn thing about homosexuals. They lived a supposedly dark, underground existence that other people never talked about. Hell, he didn't even have the faintest idea how they made love. The closest he'd ever come to their world was once in high school when a man in his thirties had winked at him on a bus. All the same, Héctor liked to think of himself as being tolerant when it came to other people's sexuality. As long as they didn't bother the normal people, they could fuck whomever and however they wanted.

And what was that supposed to mean? Who the hell were the normal people? Was Héctor normal? After having broken his two months of abstinence (not counting the two or three times he'd jerked off, and a pair of wet dreams) by making love with a teenager with a broken arm?

Belascoarán felt his horizons expanding. One thing he'd learned over the last few months was that nobody's problems were all that different from his own.

He moved on to the third photograph where Elena smiled warmly.

He posted a third sheet of paper, and wrote:

> You've got something worth 50,000 pesos.
>
> You told the fat man's friends and they tried to make you give it to them.
>
> Someone tried to kill you. (Not the fat man's friends. Someone else.)
>
> To kill you, or to scare you?
>
> Whatever it is you've got, it implicates your mother in some way.
>
> Your mother's a junkie.
>
> I've got a bad feeling about a guy named Burgos.

Héctor leaned back from the wall and gazed at the three pictures with their three pieces of paper, like someone contemplating a painting by Van Gogh. A mystery-novel detective would have shouted, "Eureka!" and everything would have fallen into place.

But appearances were often deceiving, especially when the clues were no more than bits and pieces of disconnected information pointing in no clear direction. There was, for instance, the fact that Marisa Ferrer shot smack, yet Elena's secret whatever-it-was could be anything from a set of KGB microfilms to a collection of rare postage stamps, or the key to a safe-deposit box in the Banco de Mexico with evidence implicating a cabal of bankers in a coup attempt against the previous administration.

And Burgos, in spite of the fact that he was ugly as sin and rubbed Héctor the wrong way, could turn out to be no more than a peace-loving and harmless filmmaker. By the same token, Commander Paniagua of the Judicial Police might be just another gangster dedicated to the preservation of law and order. Wasn't that the great virtue of reality over fiction, that it was significantly more complex?

Héctor yawned loudly, and the engineer smiled at him.

"Tired, huh? Seems like you've been dragging a little lately... If you keep spending your nights drawing on the wall under your pictures and your days chasing murderers, you're going to wear yourself out."

"You've got a point there."

Héctor walked across to where the broken-down armchair waited for him like a lover.

No doubt about it, life's greatest virtue was its complexity.

"Will you wake me up before you go?"

"I'll be done around five-thirty, when I finish with this mess," answered the engineer, examining a set of sewer maps that looked more like a series of drawings by Paul Klee. He lit one of his thin cigars, and blew the smoke toward the ceiling.

"Oh, I forgot to tell you, before you came in someone called on the phone and threatened to kill you."

"What'd you tell him?" asked Héctor as he made a pillow out of his jacket and tucked his gun between his body and the back of the chair.

"Oh, I gave him a piece of my mind."

"And what'd he say to that?"

"That it was none of my business and to wait and see if they didn't come after me, too."

"See what you get for getting involved?"

Héctor took off his shoes, and El Gallo Villareal went to open the window. A gust of cold air cleared the stuffiness from the room. The engineer flicked the ash of his cigar out the window, and Héctor imagined it tumbling the four stories down to the street.

"Sometimes a guy gets tired of these lousy maps," remarked the engineer, pulling a large revolver out of his jacket pocket and setting it underneath his drawing table.

"Careful now…Is the safety on? Next thing you know it'll go off and Gilberto and Carlos'll say it's my fault." The detective smiled.

"You're the one that needs to think about being careful, neighbor…"

"If there's one thing I've learned after working at this job for a year, it's that you don't run away when the threats start coming in."

"Did it ever occur to you, Belascoarán, that they might not be bluffing?"

"Yeah."

"So why don't you find yourself another line of work?"

"I guess I like this one…Yeah, I guess I must like it," he said, and shut his eyes.

The road to the factory was blocked again by police cars. Workers from other nearby factories milled around the gate, unsure whether to get involved or to go back to work.

Héctor got out of the VW and flashed his license at the cop who stopped him. The gray, dusty morning was charged with electricity. A pair of policemen sat inside each patrol car, with riot helmets and machine guns. He could hear the whinnying of horses. Almost five hundred striking workers stood in irregular rows inside the gate, sticks and stones in their hands. Behind them, the red-and-black banners. Some twenty yards away, there was a detachment of mounted police brandishing drawn swords, flanked by three patrol cars on either side. The company president sat in his car behind the squadron of horses, his engineers swarming around him. Engineer Camposanto sat in his own car, with the door open. Héctor walked past him and approached Rodríguez Cuesta.

"I can't talk to you now. Come back tomorrow," said the company president when Héctor was still six feet away.

Héctor went on past him and through the line of horses. One of the animals was taking a shit, another beat its hoofs on the ground, raising a cloud of dust. Héctor kept his gaze away from the mounted officers, afraid of breaking the spell that opened a path before him. Finally, a sergeant thrust the flat of his sword against Héctor's chest.

"Where do you think you're going?"

"I'm going through."

"Reporter?"

"Yes."

"Then you'd better stay out of the way," he said, and shoved Héctor back with his sword.

Héctor retreated. He headed across to the *lonchería*, where it sat in a sort of no-man's-land. A low, pent-up murmur started to rise from the crowd, growing in strength: "FREE THE DELEX THREE, FREE THE DELEX THREE, COPS OUT OF DELEX, COPS OUT OF DELEX." A horse whinnied.

"Are you the detective?"

Héctor nodded at his questioner, a young man about twenty years old, dressed in a factory uniform.

"What are you doing over here?" Héctor asked.

"If it gets ugly I'm supposed to call our lawyer," said the young man. He held his right fist in his left hand, squeezing it as if he were squeezing the juice from an orange.

"Is there some way I can get in there?" asked the detective.

"There's a vacant lot behind the factory where you can get through…But you'd better leave well enough alone, this doesn't have anything to do with you."

"According to who?"

"The committee…Someone said you were a friend, but you can't ever be too sure."

Héctor looked at him for a moment.

"What's going to happen here?"

"Pretty soon the people from the neighborhood will turn out, and some of the students, too, from the Polytechnic. The cops'll probably back off then. They're just waiting for their orders. From the governor, most likely. You'd better go."

But something held him there, in the door to the *lonchería*.

"What's the strike about, anyway?"

"So that they'll recognize the independent union, and let our *compañeros* out of jail. And to keep out any more scabs."

A pair of uniformed policemen left the pack of horses and approached the mass of strikers. A crowd gathered around them, and then let out a raucous shout, followed by chants and applause. The mounted police began to file away in an orderly fashion, and the president's car lurched into reverse and roared away.

"What's going on?" asked Héctor.

"They're going away. They can't beat us yet. They'll ask to negotiate, wait and see."

The young worker headed off toward the factory and Héctor slipped into the *lonchería* for a soda. It seemed his mouth was almost always dry these days. The dark interior of the restaurant soothed his tired eyes. Outside, it was a dirty, sunless morning. He took a seat, and the woman set a bright red soda on the table in front of him.

"I called your office, but no one answered."

"Thanks," Héctor said, handing her a twenty-peso note.

"What's up, shamus? Packin' a rod? Which side were you planning to use it on?" asked the fat worker, entering with his friends to celebrate their victory. He walked by Héctor and sat down at a nearby table.

Héctor tried to think of something to say, but after a while, he just gave up.

Commander Federico Paniagua, it turned out, kept a rather flexible schedule. He had a house in the Lechería neighborhood, where his old lady lived with their two grown children. The wife was fiftyish and fat, and an excellent cook (a conclusion arrived at after two hours of smelling the delicious odors wafting out of her kitchen onto the street). The commander also kept a room in an old hotel, whose green wooden doors opened onto an inner courtyard with a fountain. There he was known as Ernesto Fuentes, a traveling salesman.

He had another place as well, an apartment in a modern building in the Irrigación district, around the corner from the Mundet Country Club. No one there seemed to know anything about him. An insurance agency occupied the ground floor, and in the two apartments above the commander's there lived an old, retired British bachelor, an ex-functionary of his government's consulate in Guadalajara; and a pair of newlyweds. There was no doorman, only a woman who cleaned the stairs every other day, and a rent collector who came around once a month.

Paniagua stopped in once or twice each week at police headquarters in Tlanepantla, and made several weekly trips to Toluca.

When he was working, he was always accompanied by two men: one, his chauffeur, was always the same; and the other changed depending on the vehicle the commander used.

If Héctor were in charge of an agency with sixteen operatives at his disposal, he would have sent one to watch the apartment in Irrigación, and another to take a room in the Hotel Doncelas. But where there's a will there's a way, and he decided to spend the night keeping an eye on one or the other himself. In the meantime, he left the north end of town and drove the twenty tiring kilometers south to Marisa Ferrer's house, only to be greeted by a silent maid who shut the door in his face.

# Chapter Ten

…Breathe deeply and above all
make sure you don't drop your
gun as the ground rushes rapidly
toward your face.

—Roque Dalton

His eyes were two slits, his arms hung limply at his sides, he dragged his feet across the soft ground; his mouth was dry and bitter, and little invisible hairs grew around his teeth.

He would gladly have traded his gun for a fountain of cold, pure water where he could wash his face, revive himself, listen to the birds come to drink and the children passing by on their way to school.

For lack of a fountain, he got a maid to lend him the hose she was using to wash her employer's car, and he ran the cold water over his face until it was numb.

Shaking himself like a wet dog, he walked back to his car and ended his wasted vigil in front of the apartment building on Irrigación.

Something had to give: if he went on like this, just letting things evolve slowly on their own, he was going to end up keeled over from fatigue on some street corner, with his back to the wall and his eyes caked with sleep. It was time to stir things up. He was sick and tired of not being able to play all eleven positions at once. The ball kept passing him by, and even though he ran up and down the field the whole game, he could never make a play. The time had come to throw a wrench into the works, to make something happen.

But how to break this scoreless tie?

The sister led him to an unused classroom, with an old piano and the remains of a cardboard-and-wood stage set depicting clouds. The room had a wooden floor and was half-filled with broken chairs and desks. Héctor lit a cigarette and sat down on one of the chairs. It creaked under his weight. He hung his head and rested his elbows on his knees, allowing the cigarette to burn down on its own, glancing occasionally at the thin line of smoke that drifted lazily toward the ceiling.

"*Señor* Detective, here are the girls," said the young nun. He could see Elena's three friends waiting in the hall behind her.

"Could I have a minute with the girls alone, Sister?"

"I hope it won't take long. Their English teacher asked to have them back in class as soon as possible."

"Don't worry, it'll only take a minute."

The girls filed in, a mixture of shyness and curiosity, laughing and giggling among themselves. Héctor motioned them toward the chairs and they sat down, mechanically reaching out to pull their skirts down over their knees. Héctor thought about the girl in his bed and her jokes about the lost virginity of Catholic school girls.

"Gisela, Carolina, Bustamante…" Héctor began.

"Ana Bustamante," corrected a thin, bright-faced girl, black hair falling across one eye.

"I need your help," he said, and paused. The girls nodded.

"Is Elena all right?" one of them asked.

"She's okay right now. But if I don't find what I'm looking for, she may be in a great deal of danger."

He looked the girls in the eye, one at a time, with as much intensity as he was capable of in his exhausted condition.

"Did Elena give any of you something to keep for her?"

The girls looked at one another.

"Not me."

"Me either."

"She asked me if I could keep a package in my papa's safe, but I told her I didn't know the combination," said the girl named Bustamante.

"When was that?"

"A couple of weeks ago, before they started coming to harass her at school."

"Did she say anything else about it to any of you?"

"No," one of them answered, and the others shook their heads.

"Thanks," Héctor said.

The girls stood up and filed out of the room.

Now what? wondered the detective, slumped down in a broken-backed chair.

"Wait!" he shouted, and ran into the hall.

"Does Elena have a locker here at school?"

With the package stowed under the VW's backseat, Héctor pulled up in front of the courthouse in Santa Clara. He was in no hurry to open it now.

One third of his problems were over, and he knew that the solution, wrapped up in a small parcel of brown paper and tied with a piece of string, would wait safely in the parked car. He entered the building and roamed the halls, asking for the office of the public prosecutor in charge of the case.

"What's your business?" asked a young, dark-skinned bureaucrat wearing a loud necktie. The tie had a spot of egg yolk smeared across it.

"I've got some important information about the murder of engineer Alvarez Cerruli at the Delex plant."

"What's your name?"

"Héctor Belascoarán Shayne."

A door opened and Héctor stepped into an office where two men stood waiting.

One of them seemed like an old friend after the last few days: Commander Paniagua. He leaned against a metal file cabinet in the back of the room, with his gun showing conspicuously at his belt. The other man introduced himself as Attorney Sandoval, public prosecutor. Abandoning formalities, Héctor took a seat without waiting for an invitation.

"You say you have some information pertaining to the murder of Engineer Alvarez Cerruli?" Then, pointing to his associate, the prosecutor asked, "Do you know Commander Paniagua? He's in charge of the investigation."

Héctor said he did, and Paniagua returned a puzzled look from behind his dark glasses.

"What I've got pertains to the case, all right. It shows that you boys are barking up the wrong tree. And I can prove it." He took out his notebook and glanced at a page, letting the challenge hang in the air.

"I can prove that the men you arrested couldn't have committed the crime. The time of the murder has been set between five and five-thirty, when Gustavo Fuentes hadn't even come in for work yet. There are a number of witnesses who can testify that Ibáñez was on the assembly line from four o'clock until five-thirty. And Contreras didn't come in at all that day.

"What I'm saying is that it might be a good idea if you let them go before I decide to go to the papers and tell them how you've gotten yourselves mixed up unfairly in a labor dispute out here."

Héctor lit a cigarette and waited.

"What's your interest in all this?" asked the public prosecutor.

Héctor smiled.

◇◇◇

Scrambled eggs with ham, a pitcher of orange juice, sliced bananas and cream: it was Héctor's idea of a perfect breakfast.

"You look like a ghost," said Elisa as she set the plates on the table.

"You don't look so great yourself, Sister."

They were seated in the old family breakfast nook. Elisa, wrapped in a yellow terry-cloth bathrobe, rubbed her eyes.

"I'm tired. I was up until I don't know how late talking to your client."

"How's she doing?" Héctor asked, attacking his eggs with gusto.

"She's a bright kid. Sometimes she amazes me, other times I just feel sorry for her. I suppose I'd be pretty surprised to see myself at her age…Everything seemed so easy back then."

"Did she tell you anything?"

"Not directly, but if I knew part of the story…"

"There's your answer over there," he said pointing to the brown-paper-wrapped package. "I don't know what it is yet."

Elisa picked up the glass of orange juice Héctor poured for her and downed it in one gulp. Héctor watched her with affection.

"What have you been doing lately?" he asked.

"Going around in circles, mostly. I haven't felt right ever since I came home. I've been thinking about going back to school."

"Do you ever hear from that guy? Your ex, I mean."

"I get a letter from Alan once a month. A short note that always says the same thing, and a check for four hundred dollars that I rip up into tiny pieces and send back to him. Do you know why I got married and left Mexico?" She looked earnestly at her brother.

"Well, back then…"

"I always felt sandwiched in between you and Carlos. You were the good kid, responsible, devoted, well behaved. And Carlos was the little genius. All I wanted was to get out of the house and prove I could make it on my own. Getting married seemed like a way to do that."

Héctor reached over and squeezed her hand. Elisa smiled.

"A bad time for confession, isn't it?"

"It's always a bad time…The past stinks, it's never easy to look back. Like with Papa now. Six years after he died, and all of a sudden I realize we were never close to him, we never understood who he was. Everything was covered by a smoke screen…It was the same with you and me."

"Alan was the perfect journalist. All day long he worked at the paper, all night long he sat drinking in the bar of some lousy hotel. Do you know what Canada was like? A house set off all by itself, a color TV, you watch the snow fall in the afternoon. I used to talk to myself just to keep from losing my Spanish."

"Didn't you used to play guitar?"

"I even gave up on that. I forgot everything. It was like living in a dream, a dream turned into a nightmare. I never got so that I could understand that country, much less get free of it. *Puta madre*, it makes me sick just to think about it."

"Let it be, Elisa," Héctor soothed her. He pushed his empty plate to one side.

"Are you going to wait for her to wake up?"

"Not now. I'll be back in a couple of hours. Don't let her go anywhere."

"If you're back in time for lunch, I swear I'll be in a better mood, and I'll make us six different dishes of Chinese food."

"Hide this package where she won't find it, will you?" Héctor said, lighting a cigarette. The smoke tasted wonderful on a full stomach, and with the whole morning ahead of him.

"You said you saw Rodríguez Cuesta leave the plant? You said you remembered because he asked you to have his tire fixed, or his jack, or something?"

Security Guard Rubio, badge number 6453, nodded. Dressed in a T-shirt, a cup of coffee in his hand, he offered Héctor a seat in a damp-walled room full of plastic-covered furniture. "This is my day off, I don't work today. Understand?"

"Was he alone?"

"Yeah, he was alone in the car."

"And when he went in, earlier in the day. Was he alone then?"

"He always comes to work alone."

"Sure, but what about this time? What time did he get there?"

"Rodríguez Cuesta always comes in around ten o'clock."

"And on that day? Are you sure he was alone?"

"Just a minute. I don't think I saw him go in that day. I was checking the papers on a pickup as he drove by, and I didn't really get a good look at him. But I think he was by himself. He always comes by himself."

"Who was driving the pickup?"

"Just one of the guys from the factory—I forget his name. They call him Sleepyhead, or something like that."

"One more question...No, two more."

"Whatever you want."

"Do the engineers come to work alone?"

"Yeah, they've all got their own cars. Sometimes you'll see one of them catching a ride from someone else because his car's in the shop..."

"Was Camposanto by himself?"

"I think so."

"And when they leave their cars in the lot...?"

"They don't park in the main lot; there's a covered place for the managers' cars, with their names marked on their own private parking space."

"And is there anybody around there at that time of day?"

"Sure, if they come in early enough, some of the guys from the factory might be back there. Later on, maybe just a forklift operator, something like that."

"One last question: How many more cops came besides the first two?"

"Uh...First there was one squad car, then another one came. Then two unmarked cars, and then the ambulance."

"Was Commander Paniagua in one of those cars?"

"No. No, I didn't see him go in. I saw him leave, though. Maybe he went in the back entrance."

"The back entrance?"

"There's another gate around behind the factory, in a vacant lot where they used to take the trucks through. They keep it locked, though. I think the strikers have a guard there now."

"But how could Paniagua get through if the gate was locked?"

"Let me think about it. I'm not so sure I saw him there, after all. You're talking about the same one that arrested the three guys from the union?"

"That's the one. Short, dark, wears sunglasses, around fifty or so..."

"Well, he definitely didn't go in with the other cop cars, but he was there. I saw him leave."

"Did you see him inside the plant?"

Héctor took the same question to the secretary, to a striker keeping watch over the rear gate, to a pair of forklift operators. The striking workers regarded him with distrust and answered his questions guardedly. No one remembered seeing the policeman on the day of the murder, but some said they'd seen him there at other times.

Paniagua could be the murderer. But what was Héctor basing his suspicions on? A single anonymous phone caller who claimed that he was a homosexual? He could have gone in with Rodríguez Cuesta, in the trunk of his car, or he could have gone in through the back gate.

Did he have an alibi? And how was Héctor supposed to find out where the commander had been that afternoon? There was no point in asking the Police Department. It was just one more shot in the dark that had missed its mark. He'd have to try another angle.

◇◇◇

The first thing Héctor saw when the door opened was the gun, then he saw the fear in the man's face.

"Am I just supposed to stand here, or are you going to invite me in?" the detective asked.

"I don't want to talk to you."

"You can't be too busy these days, with the factory on strike…" Héctor said, pushing the door gently with his shoulder.

Engineer Camposanto moved to one side. Héctor walked through the oversized dollhouse and settled into a chair in the living room while Camposanto closed the door.

"There's nothing I can tell you."

Dragging his feet, the engineer walked over to Héctor's chair and set the gun on the coffee table in the center of the room. Héctor took a cigarette from his pocket and lit it. He let the lighter drop from his hand onto the floor, and when the engineer bent over to pick it up, Héctor drew his gun.

Camposanto straightened up with the lighter, only to find the gun staring him in the face.

"What do you want from me?"

"Give me your gun. Use two fingers and pick it up by the barrel, that's right…" Héctor took the gun and slipped it into his coat pocket. Camposanto sat down, sank his head between his hands, and started to cry, sobbing loudly.

Héctor looked at him uneasily, and drew on his cigarette.

"I didn't want to," the engineer sobbed.

"Then why'd you do it?" asked Belascoarán, taking a shot in the dark, like a blindfolded child swinging wildly in the air at a *piñata* dangling somewhere overhead.

"Why'd I do what?" asked Camposanto, wiping his tears away with the sleeve of his gray robe.

"Why'd you kill him?"

"I didn't kill anybody," he protested.

"Let me think a minute."

"You don't know what you're talking about."

"Maybe not, but I suppose I could beat the shit out of you until you decided to fill me in."

"Go to hell. You've got no reason to suspect me."

"Then why'd you pull a gun on me when I came to the door?"

Camposanto looked at the floor.

"How long have you known Commander Paniagua?"

"I don't know him."

"I've got time," Héctor said, taking a pack of cigarettes from his pocket and laying it on the glass-topped table.

They waited.

The tension increased in proportion to the duration of their silence. Camposanto, sunk into his armchair, avoided the detective's gaze, and occupied himself with unraveling the threads on the cord that held the robe around his waist. Now and then he directed a furtive glance at the gun in Héctor's hand. Héctor decided the wait was in his favor. The engineer seemed to have no reserves. It was a contest between the weakness of the one and the sleepiness of the other. Héctor looked at his watch: 11:57.

12:00.

12:30.

12:48.

1:45.

"What do you want?" asked a nearly unrecognizable voice coming from the engineer's lips. He rubbed his sweaty palms.

"Answers. How long have you known Commander Paniagua?"

"Only for a few months. Alvarez Cerruli introduced us at a golf club off the highway to Queretaro."

"When did you realize that he was gay?"

"Alvarez told me…I had the feeling they'd known each other for a while."

"How did they meet?"

"He said they met at a party."

"How did Paniagua seem to you when you first met him?"

"He was very quiet…but he seemed like a nice guy."

"You were drinking coffee with Fernández, from the personnel department, when the body was discovered?" Héctor changed the subject and lit another cigarette.

"That's right…What are you implying?"

"Nothing, I just asked…What were you doing between four-thirty and five-thirty that day?"

"I got back from lunch around four, four-fifteen, and had a talk with one of the accountants, over in their department. From there I went straight to the lab and I was in the lab with the guys from quality control until a quarter past five. Then on my way back to the office I stopped in to have a cup of coffee with Fernández."

His answer was direct, delivered with perhaps a little too much confidence. But there was a hole in it.

"Who did you eat lunch with?"

"In a cafe on North Insurgentes."

"What was it called?"

"I don't remember."

"You ate alone?"

"Alone."

"Let's start again: Who did you have lunch with?"

The engineer didn't answer.

"I'm not in any hurry," said Héctor, checking his watch: 1:48.

"I had lunch with Alvarez Cerruli," Camposanto blurted out. He seemed to collapse in the chair, and went on:

"He was scared, I mean scared out of his wits. He was trapped between the two of them, and he couldn't escape. I already knew what was going to happen, because he'd already asked me...I couldn't stand it anymore, watching Alvarez eat himself up with fear, while I pretended..."

If fatigue hadn't dulled his senses, Héctor would have heard the noise at the door behind his back a little sooner, but it wasn't until the door itself was forced open with a loud crack that he threw himself to the floor, taking the chair with him, and saw the flash of the pistol. He wrenched himself around into an awkward position, with his legs tangled up in the chair, and fired twice at the open door. A hand appeared holding a gun and fired one shot in Héctor's direction. The bullet slammed into the rug an inch from the detective's face. The door swung from one of its hinges. Behind him, Héctor heard the gurgling sounds of blood in Camposanto's throat, like the sound of bubbles rising in a swamp. He was drowning in his own blood. Héctor hid his legs behind a column and fired at stomach height. The shot splintered against the door and ricocheted into the hallway. There was no one there. Belascoarán got to his feet, tripped on a lamp cord, and pressed himself against the wall. Sidestepping to the door, he jumped out. The hall was empty. His heart danced a wild dance inside his chest. Inside the apartment, Camposanto lay dying.

"Who killed him?"

"Pannhiaguah," whispered the engineer, halfway to his grave.

Héctor had never liked the man, but now he was dying, and there was nothing Héctor could do. Death confused him, intimidated him.

"Sign here," he demanded, taking out his notebook and putting his pen in the dying man's hand. On the second try, Camposanto managed to steady the pen and scribble his name at the bottom of the sheet. Blood soaked through his shirt under the gray robe. Héctor took hold of his hand, and, dipping the engineer's fingers in his own blood, pressed a couple of fingerprints beside the signature. By the time he lifted the bloodied hand from the page, it belonged to a dead man. Héctor pushed it away with a mixture of fear and disgust.

Above the signature he wrote: "Commander Paniagua murdered Alvarez Cerruli," along with the date and time: 1:55.

There was blood on his hand. He wiped it on the engineer's robe.

If this was Paniagua's work, the police would be waiting in the street to arrest Héctor for the murder. Unless they were already on their way up in the elevator. Héctor raced out of the apartment. The hall was still empty, but voices could be heard behind the other doors. He leapt up the stairs. On the roof, two women were washing clothes and a boy played with a wheel-less toy car on a highway drawn with chalk. Héctor jumped over the highway, then scaled a low fence that stood between him and the roof of the neighboring building.

Back down in the street all was quiet; there were no police. Héctor walked back to his car and climbed in. He gunned the motor, and only then realized he was covered with sweat. And he wasn't tired anymore. Two questions stuck in his mind: Why kill Alvarez Cerruli at his office if it would have been just as easy to do it somewhere else? Why hadn't the murderer come in to finish Héctor off, too?

◇◇◇

The game had taken a turn for the worse—like when a little kid pokes out another kid's eye by mistake. And then he has to try to explain to the adults that he was only playing, that it was just a game and nobody meant to poke anybody's eye out, that the blood running across the floor is only paint.

He dropped his shirt on the floor and washed his hands furiously. His face reflected back at him out of the mirror, pale, yellowish, stubbly, his eyes bloodshot. Like the face of a ghost. Dammit! Three dead men, and what for?

On his cheek there was a small red mark, like a burn. Could it be from the bullet that had hit the rug a few inches from his face? he wondered.

Elisa watched him from the doorway.

"Is something wrong?"

"They killed a guy I was with."

"What happened?"

"Nothing. They killed him."

He would have liked a fresh shirt, but he picked up the one he'd discarded and put it back on. He buttoned it up clumsily while he stared at the ghost in the mirror.

"Elena's waiting for you. Do you want me to be there?"

"Yes. And bring the package I gave you."

Elena sat reading a novel on the patio, with the sun falling across her legs, and a soda pop on the ground next to her chair.

Héctor walked over to her and picked up the soda. One long swallow dissolved the lump in his throat.

"What's happening? You look like a ghost."

"Just yesterday I looked like a guardian angel."

"You're too beat-up for an angel today. Look at your face."

Elisa approached them dragging a couple of chairs. Héctor went to give her a hand.

"What's that doing here?" Elena asked when she saw the package.

"I had to go get it myself, since you wouldn't show it to me on your own."

"Are you going to open it?"

"Uh-huh."

"What are you going to do with it then?"

"You tell me."

"Nothing, how should I know? Burn it, put it back where I found it…Sell it, take the money and run…That's what started this whole horrible mess."

"Does your mother know what you've got?"

"I don't think Mama even knows they exist."

"Enough already. Why don't you just open it up and take a look," said Elisa.

"You're going to be surprised," warned Elena.

"Nothing surprises me anymore," said Héctor.

There were seventy-two clear, glossy photographs. They would have been perfect as illustrations in a national Kama Sutra, or for the inauguration of a successful school for the study of human sexuality. There was only one woman in all the photos, recognizable over and over again by the mole on her left buttock, or the distant smile emerging amidst a flurry of breasts and pubic hair. She appeared alternately with three different men, each one easily identifiable as an important political figure from an earlier administration, whose noble names once filled the newspapers, and today still appeared occasionally in ministry press releases.

Belascoarán smiled at the picture of the elastic and beautiful woman side by side with the three little gnomes, sweaty, feverish, and without grace.

"I feel so embarrassed," murmured Elena.

"This is amazing," said Elisa.

"Does your mother know these pictures exist?" asked the detective.

"She wouldn't have let them take them if she'd known about it. Maybe she's a whore, but she's still got class," said the girl, biting her lip.

Crowning the stack was a glossy of an ex-government minister pursuing a naked Marisa Ferrer across an enormous round bed. She held a pillow across her stomach, leaving her breasts to dance in the open air. All the man wore was a pair of socks.

"Where did you get these?"

"I stole them from Burgos's car...One night when he was having dinner with Mama, I broke into his car with a wire and a screwdriver. I took a box that had these pictures, a tape recorder, and some other stuff. I didn't know what I was getting, I just did it to play a joke on that idiot Burgos. I can't stand him. I dumped the tape recorder and the rest of the stuff in a vacant lot, but I kept the package to see what it was. I couldn't believe it when I opened it up; I mean I was scared. It made me feel sick."

"Was he the one who pushed you off the balcony when you broke your arm?"

The girl nodded. She was crying now, openly, without trying to hide her face, unashamed of her tears. Elisa hugged her, and stayed by her side.

"What about the second accident?" asked Héctor.

"I never knew what happened. I guess it was just a coincidence."

"What did Burgos say to you?"

"When he pushed me out of the window…I was reading, and he came into the room. I was scared of him, so I went out onto the balcony. He said he knew I had the pictures, and that I'd better give them back. I said I didn't know what he was talking about, and he pushed me. I don't think he meant to have me fall…"

Héctor let out a sigh. At least it seemed as though Burgos was the only one who knew, the sole owner of this illustrated encyclopedia of political erotica. Only Burgos, and not the political wolf pack.

"If the men in these pictures ever found out what we've got here, we'd be as good as dead. What are you, crazy? Who'd you think you were going to sell this to?"

"They're worth a lot of money."

"Yeah, right, plenty more than the 50,000 pesos it'll cost you for a piece of ground at The Little Chapel of the Chimes. Did the fat man and his friends ever have any idea what you were trying to sell them?"

"I showed them one picture with him in it."

She pointed to the top of the stack.

"I think it's time to have something to eat," said Elisa. "If we keep talking about this, I'm not going to be able to sleep for a week."

"From fear or from erotic shock?" asked Héctor, laughing.

"Both," answered Elisa.

Elena Ferrer smiled from behind her tears.

◇◇◇

He had snoozed away the rest of the afternoon in a movie theater, stalling for time and regathering his energies. Now, while he devoured an elaborate sundae made with six different flavors of ice cream, nuts, whipped cream, fresh strawberries, melon, and cherry syrup, he sketched his thoughts on a paper napkin:

> a) How did Paniagua get into the plant?
>    Why did he kill Alvarez Cerruli?
>    Why does R.C. want proof against Paniagua?
> b) Where did the old man go after he quit the market in '66? Caves?
> c) Photos: Destroy them? Sell them?
>    What about Burgos?

He savored the last spoonfuls of ice cream, no less enjoyable for all their sickly sweetness. His personal theory was that the more complicated the dish of ice cream, the more calories it contained. Now it seemed to him that even if things had become a whole lot clearer than they were before, it was with a particularly dense and impenetrable brand of clarity.

Evening fell over the city as Héctor stretched his stiff legs. He walked along Insurgentes through the waves of rush-hour traffic: office workers in their mass exodus, fleeing homeward like the chosen people, myriads of teenagers asserting their control over the streets, cars, cars, and more cars tooting out the sorrowful car-horn symphony.

It was all very familiar to Héctor, who had been both witness and accomplice to this same scene many times before.

The labyrinth's paths all lead to the center. To the plaza of human sacrifice?

Through the Land of the Minotaur, through the butcher's playground, the three stories marched finally toward the finale.

*Finally toward the finale.* He liked the way that sounded. Resuming his role as the solitary hunter, Héctor pushed his numbed body down the sidewalk, amidst the bewildering roar of traffic, searching for the threads that would lead him to the surprising finale.

The first thing was to find a way out of the Delex mess. A way out without playing into the hands of either the murderous police commander or the omnipotent company president. And a way out of Burgos's photo-pornographic imbroglio.

That at least seemed straightforward enough, but something tugged persistently at the back of his mind. What had the fat worker said in the *lonchería*, his words beating like a club at Héctor's unconscious until the detective finally sat up and took notice: "Packin' a rod, shamus…"

Burgos was like a little flea taking pictures of naked gnome-like politicians in a society that had institutionalized the idea of an artist's career as one long bed-hopping marathon. It was a country where power was won and held at cock point. The big fuckers carve up the spoils while the rest of us look on.

And if Burgos was a mere flea, then Paniagua was a routine and expedient functionary. One thing about Paniagua: he played outside the normal rules of the game, he lived his life on the edge of the system. But that's just the kind of man the system turned to when it decided it was time to murder some more students or crack down on the independent trade unions.

Out of all of them, the only one that really seemed out of place in the Mexican landscape was Héctor himself. Maybe that's why they wanted to kill him. And maybe it wouldn't be such a hard thing to pull off, after all.

A loner like me, he thought, dies without making a sound. Nothing changes in the big picture when he's gone.

He pulled up in front of Marisa Ferrer's house, threw the butt of his cigarette out the window, and breathed in the cool night air. Flowers. He could smell flowers somewhere. What kind? He'd never been able to tell one from another. Looking around he spotted some white flowers climbing a trellis. Rosebushes bloomed in front of the house next door. If he'd bothered to look over his shoulder he would have seen two men getting out of a newly painted salmon-colored Rambler station wagon.

"Put your hands where we can see them, buddy," said a voice at his back.

Héctor turned slowly, with his hands at his sides. He'd ridden in the car with the window open and his jacket buttoned up. It would take him forever to get at his gun.

The fat man stepped toward him, waving a knife in one hand. Just behind him was the young man who, earlier in this same story, had thrown the pop bottles at the girl's feet. He held a .22 automatic. Esteban, was that his name? Esteban *Greenjacket*?

"Well, if it isn't the fat man, good to see you…and Esteban, I don't think we've met."

"Shut the fuck up," commanded the fat man.

"We want the pictures," said Esteban, pointing the gun at Héctor's face.

If the fat man moves in front of him, then…thought Héctor momentarily. But that kind of heroics was better left to the movies. Before he ever got to the fat man the kid would have blown off half his face.

"I don't have any pictures."

"Yeah, but she's got them. You think you're pretty tough. You like to talk big…"

Héctor smiled. Silence was perhaps his only weapon.

The fat man kicked him in the shin. He'd obviously picked up a thing or two from Héctor. The surprise attack, the art of striking out of nowhere. Héctor stumbled and fell, and the fat man kicked him in the ribs. Héctor's shout never made it past his lips. Esteban *Greenjacket* ground his foot onto Héctor's ankle and Héctor screamed. Geraniums. Were they geraniums? The white flowers. Irises? Lilies? Orange blossoms? No, orange blossoms only grow on orange trees. The fat man let fly with a kick to the stomach. Héctor felt the air rush out of his lungs. It didn't want to go back in, and Héctor fought against the feeling of suffocation, as the fat man ran his knife down the sleeve of Héctor's jacket. The sharp steel pricked his skin and blood spurted out.

"That'll teach you not to fuck with us."

"What's going on? I'm going to call the police!" cried a woman's voice from somewhere down the street. The fat man and Esteban *Greenjacket* left Héctor where he lay and sprinted to their car. Héctor watched the dark boots pound the grass beside the sidewalk. Fighting to draw a breath, he heard the car start and pull away. His rescuer's legs appeared before him, protruding from the bottom of her skirt.

"Thangdz," he muttered.

"I was wondering when I was going to see you again," said Marisa Ferrer, smiling at him from a hundred yards overhead. Héctor pressed his cheek against the grass, wishing he were still dozing in the movie theater, wishing he hadn't abandoned Tarzan just as he was about to cross the dangerous mountain pass. All for a lousy dish of ice cream and some rotten flowers.

"Where's the room with the round bed?" asked the detective.

She sat on a stool, her back to the oval-mirrored dressing table, looking at him with amusement.

I'll never get used to looking at this woman with her clothes on, he thought. A pair of bedside lamps emitted a soft light through their blue shades, and the blue-carpeted room seemed to go on forever without beginning or end. It was like being on the inside of an egg.

"The round bed…It's not here?"

"Did they kick you in the head, too?"

Héctor shook his head.

"Is Elena all right?" she asked softly, smiling.

She's all right but you're a lot better, he thought, but he just nodded his head at the woman and stretched out on her bed.

"She's not hurt, is she?"

"No, don't worry, she's fine…You made love in a room with a round bed…"

"I suppose I have once or twice…You don't get to be my age without having seen a thing or two…" She made a gesture that left her words hanging in the air, and then brought her hands back gracefully to her sides.

"A round bed. Was it in a rented house, or what? Where was it?"

"You're serious?"

"Totally. You took a little roll in the hay with some big-time politicians, government ministers. Somebody took pictures. And if certain people find out about those pictures, you can kiss your sweet ass good-bye. Where was it?"

"That's not possible."

"I've seen the pictures."

Marisa Ferrer went over to the night table and got her cigarettes. She lit one.

"Pass me the lighter, will you?"

With his good arm, Héctor took a crumpled pack of Delicados from his shirt pocket. The actress held out a gold lighter and lit his cigarette. They stared at each other through the flame.

"Does Elena know about it?"

Héctor nodded.

"What does she think of me?"

"I don't know."

"And you?"

"It gets harder all the time for me to judge...I wouldn't have done it myself," he said, meaning it as a joke.

"Sometimes you feel like an old glove...At first it makes you feel sick to use your body. They always told you it wasn't something to play with. But you wash it off and it's as good as new, better even. And so you keep on going...pursuing your career without having to starve yourself, taking revenge on the friends from high school who called you a whore, and on your aunt in Guadalajara who won't talk to you anymore. And walking over the rest of them. Have you heard that line before, about walking over the rest of them? I said it in *Flower of Evil*...another stupid movie. And it doesn't do any good now to cry and say you're ashamed. Sure, I'm ashamed. God, how ashamed I feel. Weren't there other men? Gentler, more honest, more human, less screwed up…with less money, less power…Sooner or later you find out even they've got nothing to give you. And still I've got this."

She spoke her words without looking at the detective, half turned away, part profile, with her beautiful, gentle face, periodically contorted with rage, outlined against the bluish light. Héctor lay on the bed, aching all over, wishing he could take off his shoes, turn on the TV, and change the channel, like someone changing lives. He looked around for somewhere to put the ash from his cigarette. He didn't feel like hearing about her problems; he didn't want to try to understand. He just wanted to be left alone.

Marisa Ferrer stood up, tore the straps off her dress, and reaching around her back, but calmer now, attuned to the established rhythm, lowered the zipper and let the dress slide over her hips and onto the floor. Her breasts glowed in the soft lamplight. She wore only a tiny pair of white panties and her black leather boots, shiny as cat fur.

Héctor was tempted to reach his hand out and touch her soft skin. The woman rolled the panties down her legs and dropped them on the floor.

"Do I scare you?"

Héctor held out his hand, and the woman stretched out at his side, naked except for the boots, abandoning the striptease that had suddenly failed because it left her irrevocably, undeniably human.

She pressed herself to his side, and Héctor hugged her to him silently. Staring up at the ceiling, he exhaled a lungful of smoke. Solidarity was all he had left to give her. Solidarity from one screwed-up human being to another, here in this country where we live and die, that takes us in, and sends us out again on our own, leaving us like carrion for the vultures. He kept his eyes fixed on the formless ceiling, the rising column of smoke.

"What a scene." She got up from the bed, and walked across to the closet to put on a robe.

Héctor thought about reaching out to stop her, but he lay there hypnotized, watching her move away.

"How are you doing?" she asked on her way back.

"Rotten."

"Let me fix your arm for you. It's not very deep, but you should probably see a doctor. You might need a few stitches."

"Where's the round bed?" Héctor asked.

◇◇◇

Belascoarán climbed into his car, and while it warmed up, he turned on the radio.

*Hello, sleepless friends. Is it really all that bad?*

The voice of El Cuervo Valdivia emerged from the rear speakers.

"No, it's worse," mumbled Héctor Belascoarán Shayne.

*Quit taking yourself so seriously…Do you think I'm here talking to you for my health? You're not the only one that has to work for a living.*

"That's right," said the detective as he put the car in gear. He braced his injured arm against the window. Now it didn't hurt so much as the pit of his bruised stomach and the leg he used on the clutch. He pulled onto Insurgentes and pointed the VW to the north, glancing here and there at apartment windows where light bulbs flickered off above late-night lovers. He imagined warm beds, a glass of milk on the night table, the last word spoken on the last movie on TV.

*Today was as bad for me as it was for you. I even thought about putting a bullet through my head…*

*But then I remembered I had a date for tonight with my brothers and sisters of the shadows, the last human beings on earth, the desperadoes, the lonely ones…So here I am again, sharing and learning in the night. Solidarity out of the solitude.*

*Why do I bother to talk about such sad things? It's because I want to share a little bit of everything with you, brothers and sisters.*

"You ought to go have a little chat with a lonely movie star I know," Héctor suggested out loud to this Valdivia whose voice came out of the radio speakers in the fluorescent darkness.

> *I've got a couple of urgent messages before I get back to the music. First of all, will the owner of a dog at one seven-five or one seven-seven Colima please put the poor animal out of its misery. It's been howling nonstop for two hours and there are five students trying to study for tomorrow's exam.*
>
> *The second message goes out to our good friend the independent detective. He's bound to be roaming around out there somewhere, caught up in the clutches of this black and beautiful night. I've had two calls in here from somebody threatening to kill you. You probably get this kind of thing every other day, but I've got the calls on tape if you're interested.*
>
> *Take it easy, buddy.*
>
> *Now, in memory of what didn't happen to me today, and in dedication to our lonely friend the detective, a special samba from Argentina.*
>
> *"The Samba Not to Die By."*
>
> *This is El Cuervo Valdivia, with the only show on the radio that mere words cannot express.*

"*My voice will break the quiet afternoon...*" began the samba. Héctor stopped the car at the corner of Insurgentes and Felix Cuevas, listening to the song.

Fifteen minutes later he pulled up in front of his office.

"What's happening, neighbor?"

The inevitable, the eternal, Engineer El Gallo Villareal sat hunched over his drawings.

"Don't you ever get bored with that stuff?"

"You betcha," answered the engineer, pausing between each syllable.

"Any messages?"

"Nope. What brings you around here this time of night?"

"I've got to check something I stowed in the 'safe' on day one."

"Day one of what?"

"Day one of this whole mess," Héctor explained, taking a soda pop out of the secret compartment, along with the file from Delex that had introduced him to the case of Alvarez Cerruli.

"I've got something for you," said El Gallo, holding out a sheaf of photocopied pages.

"What's that?"

"The other day, after you asked me about what could put the fear of God into the Delex crowd, I took a look at your notes, and then talked it over with some buddies of mine in the government. This is what I came up with."

The report was titled *Illegal Traffic in Precious Metals*, and was dated a year and a half earlier.

"This is it," concluded the detective, after reading several pages.

"That's the feeling I had when I got my hands on it."

"I owe you one, neighbor."

The engineer looked up from his maps for the first time.

"Look at you," he exclaimed. "You're a mess."

"Nothing a couple of aspirin won't cure."

Héctor turned back to the file. Now all that was left were a few loose ends to tie up, debts to collect.

Carefully he read through the testimony of the various witnesses, the secretaries, the policemen from squad cars 118 and 76, security guard Rubio. It all added up. What had Camposanto said before he died?

"I ALREADY KNEW WHAT WAS GOING TO HAPPEN, BECAUSE HE'D ALREADY ASKED ME..."

So the murdered engineers had threatened to blow the whistle on Rodríguez Cuesta's operation and the policeman had killed them. Out of greed. And to cover his own ass.

All that was left was to find out where, at which one of his three addresses, Commander Paniagua kept the picture of the dead man's wife. The macabre trophy. That should be easy enough.

"I'm going home and get some rest, neighbor."

"What about your chair?"

"This body wants a nice soft bed."

He left the smiling engineer to his maps and his thin cigars. The light had gone out again in the hallway, and only a dim glow filtered through the glass on the office door. The detective lit his cigarette lighter, and held it up beside the metal shingle:

HÉCTOR BELASCOARÁN SHAYNE: DETECTIVE

GILBERTO GÓMEZ LETRAS: PLUMBER

"GALLO" VILLAREAL: SEWER AND DRAINAGE SPECIALIST

CARLOS VARGAS: UPHOLSTERER

He held the lighter a moment longer and fired up a cigarette. Every city gets the detective it deserves, he thought.

The first burst of machine-gun fire shattered the glass on the office door and splintered the detective's right femur. With the second blast he felt as if his head were exploding into a thousand pieces. As he fell to the floor, he brought his hand up, in an absurd and pointless reflex, toward his gun. He lay bleeding on the floor, with his hand on his heart.

# Chapter Eleven

It's nothing to do with brute force.
This is a game of intellect.

—George Habasch
(reported by Maggie Smith)

"After a couple of months you ought to be able to throw the cane away. If you don't rush yourself, I think that little by little you'll regain full use of your leg. As far as your left eye goes, however, you shouldn't harbor any illusions. Some of my colleagues suggested the possibility of an operation in Switzerland…but, to be entirely frank, you've lost all sight in the eye, and the eye is dead, *Señor* Shayne."

"Belascoarán Shayne," said a hoarse voice from the chair opposite the doctor.

"*Señor* Belascoarán. Excuse me."

"Do you think you can get me a black patch, Doc? I don't like having to look in the mirror at my dead eye, as you call it."

"Of course. You can pick one up right away at the orthopedic dispensary."

Héctor limped out of the doctor's office, leaning heavily on a black cane with a curved handle. All in all, his appearance had improved significantly. A black patch over his left eye, a stubbly beard, and a cane which, with a little modification, could be engineered to hide a stiletto blade, like that of the Count of Monte Cristo.

Returning to the room where he'd spent the last three weeks, he tossed his books and pajamas into a small, plaid suitcase, slipped his gun into its holster, and hung it carefully around his shoulder.

He drew the gun again and checked the chambers and the safety. Then, dropping down onto the bed, he picked up the latest letter from the woman with the ponytail. He took his last cigarette from the bedside table, crumpled the empty pack in his hand, and tossed it at the wastebasket. He missed by a mile. Have to get used to judging distance with only one eye, he thought.

I'll have to throw a big party for your two buddies the plumber and the upholsterer. Thanks to their strange letters I know that you're getting better, even though you still aren't well enough to write. They sent me several wonderful letters that began with things like: "Dearest pony-tailed *señorita*, greetings from Carlos and Gilberto, the loyal friends and neighbors of Héctor the detective…"

They also sent newspaper clippings.

I see you finally made the headlines.

How are you?

I'm coming home. But don't think it's to be a nurse to this strange character who goes around leaving pieces of himself all over the neighborhood. No, the truth is, my search is over. And there was nothing at the end of the road. Nothing, that is, except a starlit night on the terrace of an Athens hotel spent putting off the advances of a German diplomat and an American Army captain on his NATO tour of duty.

With a quadruple iced crème de menthe in my hand. A sad ending to my quest. So at eleven P.M. I went out to find a travel agent that was still open and made reservations from here to Paris and from there on to Mexico.

I'll give you an extra week after this letter gets there, so you've got time to get used to the idea.

Here's a list of the Visigoth Kings of Spain. You be the detective, and underline the names of the murderers:

Alarico, Ataúlfo, Sigerico, Valia, Teodoredo, Turismundo, Teodorico, Eurico, Alarico II, Gasaleico, Amalarico, Teudis, Teudiselo, Agila, Atangildo, Liuva, Leovigildo, Recaredo, Liuva II, Viterico, Gundemaro,

Sisebuto, Recaredo II, Shintila, Sisenando, Kintila, Tulgo, Kindasvito, Recesvinto, Vamba, Ervigio, Egica, Vitiza, Akila, and Rodrigo.

How'd you do? If you failed to underline even one, then you blew it. This bloody bunch of hoodlums murdered thousands of people in their time.

There's a butterfly sleeping on my windowsill.

I love you,

ME.

A note was written in pencil in the margin: Iberia flight 727 from Paris, Wed. 16th. He smiled, and crumpling the letter in his hand, tossed it at the wastebasket. It hit the rim, hung there for a moment, and fell in. With this first small victory behind him, he got up and left the hospital.

◇◇◇

"You're going to drive yourself crazy, boss," said Gilberto, adding up an elaborate bill for unplugging a customer's sink.

"What is there about fixing a drain that takes you half an hour to figure out the bill?" asked the upholsterer, who had turned the classified section of *Ovaciones* into his portable bible.

Héctor was stuffing his briefcase with the files and papers dating back to the beginning of his involvement in the three mysteries. He left the photographs stuck up on the wall as a final clue in case everything else went wrong. Then he got out the sticks of dynamite.

"The cave could be right here in Mexico City," he said out loud. "Who says it's got to be in Morelos?" He picked up the telephone, and dialed a number.

"Carlos? Have you got any friends who know their way around the worst parts of town?"

◇◇◇

He was surprised to discover the priest didn't dress in the traditional uniform. He was a young man, wearing thick-lensed glasses and a gray turtleneck frayed at the elbows, with unkempt hair.

"Caves? I know of a couple, but I suppose there could be a lot more. Do you want me to ask the *compañeros* for you?"

Héctor nodded and the priest went out. The sun shone through the broken window of the parish office. A pair of posters hung on the wall: "CHRISTIANS FOR SOCIALISM." "THE WORD OF GOD HAS THE POWER TO LIBERATE THE PEOPLE OR TO PUT THEM TO SLEEP. HOW ARE WE GOING TO USE IT?"

"One of the *compañeros* suggested a third place," said the priest, coming back into the room. "I haven't been there myself, but..."

Héctor offered the priest a cigarette, and they smoked together in silence.

"Thanks a million," said Héctor, getting up. The priest handed him a small piece of paper with directions.

"Don't mention it. I remember what you did for us in that scandal over the Basilica..."

◇◇◇

"I couldn't see any reason to keep her here...What would you have done?"

Héctor shrugged his shoulders.

"She wanted to go, but she felt helpless by herself, powerless. Her mother said, 'Here's the plane ticket, let's go away together and start over again...' It seemed like the best thing..."

"The best thing..." Héctor repeated.

"You know something? You're looking pretty handsome, brother."

Héctor smiled, and raised a hand to order another espresso.

All he retained from the weeks prior to the machine-gunning was the feeling that he'd been overwhelmed by sleepiness, and this new habit of drinking cup after cup of strong coffee.

"Where'd they go?"

"Poland, I think. She got herself a grant to work in the Polish theater, and Elena was all excited about studying graphic design. She signed a piece of her cast for you and left it at the house."

Héctor paid the bill and stood up.

"What are you going to do now?"

"Collect on some debts."

"Is there anything I can do to help?"

Héctor shook his head and limped away.

"They broke the strike about three days after you went into the hospital—with the cops charging in on horses, the whole shooting match. They brought their scabs in, but our men refused to go back to work for fear of reprisals. So the company agreed not to take any action against the organizers, and everyone went back to work. Of course, the struggle goes on inside. It ebbs and flows. There were a couple of guys got fired the other day…"

"Do you see it as a defeat?" asked Héctor.

"Well…the people have to learn from the struggle. That's the only way to do it. It wasn't a victory, that's for sure, but in this town, it takes a lot of work…I don't know what to say, exactly. It wasn't a victory or a defeat…" explained Carlos. He handed Héctor a cup of steaming, strong coffee.

"Not one or the other…" said Héctor.

"Elisa put the money in the bank, under all three of our names. What do you want to do with it?"

"I wasn't planning on doing anything with it."

"What do you think if I take some of it to help the families of the men who lost their jobs?"

"Fine with me. Did they let those guys out of jail?"

"The day after they broke the strike."

"That's something, at least," said Héctor, burning his lips on the steaming coffee.

"Did you ever figure out who killed the engineer?"

"I know who, why, and how. It was no big deal, just a matter of putting all the facts together."

He got off the bus, balancing carefully on his cane, and walked toward the three-story building. Three men were pitching pennies in the street in front of an auto-parts shop.

"Got room for one more?"

They looked him over from head to toe, and smiled among themselves.

"Sure. Why not."

Héctor went first, but his coin fell more than half a foot short of the line drawn across the pavement. He lost his first peso.

The second time, Héctor's coin took a bad roll and he lost again.

On his third try, the coin fell right on the line and skipped barely half an inch. He gathered up the coins, thanked the men with a nod, and walked into the apartment building.

"He's not bad for a guy with only one eye," observed one of the men.

Héctor pushed the bell. The butler (from the way he looked he couldn't have been anything else) opened the door.

"Is Lord Kellog in?" Like cornflakes, Héctor thought. What a name.

"Who should I say is calling?"

"Héctor Belascoarán Shayne, independent investigator."

"Just a minute, please."

Through the half-open door Héctor could hear the tired footsteps of the old diplomat.

"*Sí?*" he asked in a perfectly accented Spanish, with a slightly academic, impersonal tone to it.

"I'd like you to come with me on a small piece of business. I'm going to break the law, and I want you and your butler here to be my witnesses."

"*With pleasure,*" he said excitedly in English, and called the butler: "Germinal!"

The butler returned promptly. That was the good thing about the English; you didn't need to waste a lot of time with useless explanations. The three of them went down together to the second floor. Héctor took out his gun, and shot a couple of times at the lock on the door; the flying splinters nearly tore his hand off. The lock gave way, and Héctor pushed the door open with his cane and stepped inside.

The Englishman followed, with the butler close behind. The old man shuffled his feet, and his eyes gleamed mischievously behind thick glasses. Héctor pushed open the door to the bedroom. Inside there was a large bed, a chest of drawers, a bookshelf with stacks of old magazines instead of books, a table with a single drawer. Héctor hesitated, then slid the drawer open. The photograph of Alvarez Cerruli's ex-wife smiled obligingly at him from inside its silver frame, as if she were proud of the detective's triumph.

"Now I want you to briefly write down what you've just seen, and sign it. Make a copy for yourselves."

"May I see some identification?"

Héctor showed him his wrinkled license from the Mexican Academy. They'd probably send him a new one for ten bottle caps and a couple of pesos. He could have a new picture put on it, eye patch and all.

The old Brit took out a gold fountain pen and sat down at the table. He wrote out his testimony in a large, regular script, included the date, and signed it at the bottom. The butler signed it as well.

"Thanks very much. You've been a big help."

"Let me know if I can be of any further assistance, *Señor...*"

"Belascoarán Shayne."

"Shayne?"

"My mother was Irish."

"Ah..." said Lord Kellog.

"I was sorry to hear about your..." began Rodríguez Cuesta in the comfortable shadowy dimness of his office. But Héctor interrupted him, waving the handle of his cane.

"Here's the proof that Commander Paniagua killed Alvarez Cerruli."

He tossed the files onto the president's desk. Then he dropped the piece of paper with Camposanto's bloodstained signature. It drifted lazily through the air. Finally, he slid the sheet of testimony from Lord Kellog and the butler across the desktop.

I don't know what to say, *Señor* Shayne. I thought…"

"*Señor* Cuesta, you make me sick…" Héctor said. Standing up, the detective reached over and hit him as hard as he could in the jaw with his cane. He heard the jawbone break with a clean *crack*. The company president was thrown backward, his head bouncing off the back of his black leather chair. He spit blood. A tooth fell out of his mouth.

"Tell them you tripped over the lamp cord…" said Héctor, using his cane to knock a picture of the Delex executive board off the desk.

◇◇◇

Because happy endings weren't made for Mexico. And because he had a sort of juvenile love for pyrotechnics. Héctor was pushed by these, and other, more obscure motivations, toward the finale. There was his idea that everything ought to end under the sign of the bonfire. So the Belascoarán Tribe, with its one and only member, could dance around the flames. It was his way of collecting on a dead eye and a bum leg. It was the best end to so much garbage.

He waited patiently outside the Florida Bowl, until the last of its customers had gone home for the night, discussing the strikes they could have had if that one last pin had gone down, or the lucky shot that cleared the two split pins for a spare.

He kept his eyes on the salmon-colored Rambler station wagon with the stolen plates, and imagined the fat man sitting in his squalid little room at the back of the bowling alley. The fat man, *Armgrabber*, and Esteban *Greenjacket*, talking about how close they'd come to making their stake, to literally rolling in the dough, devalued or not, and how many women, cars, hotel rooms; how much good food, U.S.A., dope, rock 'n' roll it could have bought them.

He waited until the night had fully established its control over the scene, then got out of the car. The lonely glow of his cigarette stood out in the empty street. Lovingly, he placed the stick of dynamite underneath the Rambler and lit the fuse with the tip of his cigarette. He backed away slowly, accepting the risk, playing with it.

He got back in his VW and started the engine.

The explosion filled the street, lifting the station wagon high into the air and blowing it to pieces, and shattering the newly installed windows on the front of the Florida Bowl.

A green Renault parked behind the Rambler was also destroyed in the blast. Héctor thought about it with a twinge of conscience as he drove away. He hoped that it belonged to the fat man or one of his buddies.

"War is war," he said, smiling broadly and with satisfaction.

At a public phone, he pulled over and dialed the police.

"Someone just blew up a stolen station wagon in front of the Florida Bowl. There's a dangerous mob of car thieves inside the bowling alley, so hurry…" and he hung up.

◇◇◇

The address in the Pedregal neighborhood that Marisa Ferrer gave him on the night of the machine-gunning corresponded to a large feudal castle of cold stone on a lonely street. A tall iron fence surrounded the grounds, where trees dropped their dry leaves on the wide lawn. This is going to be a regular commando job, he thought, amused. He lit a cigarette, and stuck the two remaining sticks of dynamite under his belt. Unbuttoning his jacket, he undid the safety on his gun.

"This is it!" he shouted.

The first stick of dynamite twisted the iron fence as if it were made out of coat hangers.

Héctor ran limping through the trees. A shadow emerged from the doorway, gun in hand, and the detective shot low without stopping to think. The man's gun spit fire inches from Héctor's head. Héctor ran past the man where he lay clutching his wounded leg, and kicked his revolver out of reach.

This was a new kind of game, with a whole new set of rules. Now on to second base, he thought, firing a couple of warning shots into the air.

He ran into a lamp, tripped and rolled to the floor. From there he watched a pair of naked women run past him and shut themselves in a bathroom.

Héctor pounded on the bathroom door with his cane:

"Open up!" he shouted, "I have to take a piss."

Without waiting for an answer, he ran through the house, dragging his leg, looking for the room the women had come out of. A man stood inside it, pulling on his pants, his back to the door.

"Excuse me," said Héctor.

The man dropped to the floor.

There it was, the round bed that had caused him so many sleepless nights in the hospital. And if the bed was there, the pictures must have been taken from…over there! A giant mirror filled the entire length of one wall.

He looked for a second at his reflection and then fired three shots into the mirror, which crumbled into a million shining pieces. Behind it was an elaborate photographic studio, filled with cameras and strange gadgets, even a 16-millimeter movie camera mounted on a tripod. Burgos stood in his shirtsleeves, staring disconsolately at the detective.

The man on the floor stared with eyes like saucers.

"Better run," warned Héctor, lighting the final stick of dynamite and lobbing it into the studio. "In twenty seconds this place is history."

The photographer and the naked gentleman, his pants still only half on, overtook Héctor in their rush to escape.

The wounded guard in the doorway had dragged himself almost within reach of his gun, so Héctor gave it another kick as he raced by. Then all hell broke loose behind him. Bursts of flame licked at the trees closest to the house. The two women came running out the doorway, naked.

"Hell of a party," Héctor mumbled. His car waited for him in the street, with the engine still running.

"Safe," he called out, as he slid in and shut the door.

◇◇◇

He sipped a hot cup of weak coffee in a Doni-Donut Shop on Insurgentes, served by a melancholy and pimple-faced waiter who apologetically offered him a plate of shriveled doughnuts. The young man gladly accepted one of the detective's cigarettes, and stood chatting for a minute about his favorite fighters.

Héctor had to admit to himself that he wouldn't play the same game again, not even for a million pesos. His heart beat wildly in his chest, and he could feel the fear inside his belly, more so now because he'd held it back before.

What, after all, had he accomplished? Now the fat man and his buddies would have to carry their cases of soda pop by hand and ride the Metro until they could find themselves another set of wheels. And Burgos would have to retire temporarily from the world of artistic photography. Héctor could still see the young women's rosy butts bobbing across the lawn. He wondered who the half-naked customer could have been.

The waiter brought over a couple more wrinkled doughnuts to help celebrate the detective's raucous laughter.

Later on, Belascoarán walked over to the offices of Radio 1000.

Inside the sound booth, behind the pane of glass, El Cuervo Valdivia was telling the story of the fall of the Holy Roman Empire, but with a strange personal twist. He winked at Héctor and signaled for him to wait.

Héctor relaxed in an armchair in the hall and put the finishing touches on his plan.

He walked into the police station with a portable radio under his arm, using his cane to clear a path before him. He limped more than before, with his leg feeling the effects of the previous night's activities.

"Commander Paniagua?"

A uniformed officer pointed him toward the commander's office.

Héctor walked in without knocking. Seven or eight plain-clothes cops sat at a round table drinking coffee and eating pastry.

"Excuse me," said the detective as he looked around for an outlet for the radio. He found the correct station and turned the volume all the way up.

"What's going on?" asked a man he recognized as Paniagua's chauffeur.

"Commander Paniagua?"

"He's in the can...Who the hell are you?"

"An acquaintance. Tell him to hurry up, they're going to talk about him on the radio."

As he was leaving the room Héctor bumped into the commander. They stood staring at each other momentarily. Héctor felt the fear crawling up his spine.

"One question, Commander: Were you comfortable lying down in the backseat of Camposanto's car when he sneaked you into the factory the day of the murder?"

Héctor smiled and walked away.

That was the moment Paniagua could have pulled his gun and shot him down. Héctor could feel the exact spot in his back where the bullet would enter. Behind him, in the room, the radio projected El Cuervo Valdivia's slow, dry, penetrating voice.

> *...It's a story you might hear any day. The story of how Federico Paniagua, a commander of the Judicial Police in the State of Mexico, killed three men so that he could go on blackmailing a large corporation...*

He left the brown-paper package with the editor of *Gent* magazine.

"Go ahead and print them if you dare," he said as he left. "Or maybe you can sell them to a magazine in England or France. Or stick them up your ass..."

When he thought about it, it seemed to Héctor that he'd gotten away with as much as any of the others. Hadn't he thrown sticks of dynamite, shot down gunmen, blown up station wagons, without having anything happen to him in return?

He was almost ready to accept the upholsterer's dictum, heard over and over again in their shared office: "In Mexico nothing ever happens, and even if something does, still nothing happened."

Even if Paniagua went to jail in the midst of a colossal scandal, he'd still get out two years later once the dust settled. And Burgos would go back into business sooner or later because there would always be politicians who wanted a fancy piece of ass, and there would always be actresses willing to hop from bed to bed in the name of their careers. And the problem of the photographs would be solved with enough money. Really, all Héctor had done was to make another middleman a little richer. Rodríguez Cuesta would recover from his broken jaw and continue his smuggling operation. And more gay men would be driven undercover and forced to hide their identities in a society that wasn't ready to accept them for who they were. And the dead men would always be just that, dead men rotting in lonely graves. And the strike was broken, and Zapata would always have died on the ranch in Chinameca.

The cave had electric lights. A low green wooden railing propped up with stones stood at the cave's mouth as a sort of doorway. A threadbare red curtain made a second door. Between the two, an empty bird cage hung from the stone.

"May I come in?"

"Come in, come in," said a reedy old voice.

"*Buenas noches.*"

"Likewise," answered the old man, leaning back on his cot. He wore a tattered old army blanket over his shoulders. His boots were set to one side of the straw pallet.

"I'm looking for a man," began Héctor, trying to penetrate the shadows with his one good eye.

"Could be you've found him."

"Folks around here say you go by the name of Sebastián Armenta."

"That's me."

The old man's eyes pierced him. Were these the damp, penetrating eyes of Emiliano Zapata? The same eyes sixty years later, stripped of their hopes and aspirations?

"The man I'm looking for was driven out of Morelos back in 1919. They didn't want him around anymore."

"There might be something in that...It was the government that didn't want him around."

"Then he turned up in Tampico in '26 with a young Nicaraguan named Sandino."

"He was a great man, General Sandino, a leader of free men," said the old man.

"During those years he smuggled guns for the Nicaraguans, on a boat called the *Tropical*."

"Actually they used three boats in all. There was the *Superior*, and the *Foam*, too. They were good little boats, they were..."

"He called himself Zenón Enríquez and he was a captain in Sandino's army."

"Captain Enríquez. They called him The Quiet One...that's right."

"Then in 'thirty-four, he went through Costa Rica and registered for a Mexican passport under the name of Isaías Valdez."

"Isaías Valdez," the old man repeated, as if in confirmation.

"In 'forty-four he worked as a fruit seller in the Dos de Abril Market. He was called Eulalio Zaldívar, and was close friends with Rubén Jaramillo."

"A good friend to a great *compañero*, a real man of the people. Maybe one of the last..."

"He left the market in 'forty-seven but came back fifteen years later in nineteen sixty-two, only to leave for good in 'sixty-six. In nineteen sixty-six he went back to Olivar de los Padres, took back his old name of Isaías Valdez, and lived off what he made braiding horse leads."

"He was in Morelos from nineteen forty-seven to nineteen sixty-two."

"Then in nineteen seventy, an old man named Sebastián Armenta, just like yourself, came here to live in this neighborhood.

He settled into his cave, and now he makes his living selling sweets at the entrance to the movie theaters on Avenida Revolución. Coconut candies, *alegrías*, that kind of thing."

"That's right."

"Do you know where I can find the man I'm looking for?"

The old man sat in silence. Héctor offered him a cigarette from his pack of Delicado filters. The old man took one, bit off the filter, placed the cigarette between his lips, and waited for Héctor to give him a light. Then he took a deep drag, and exhaled the smoke toward the ceiling of the cave.

"You're looking for Emiliano Zapata," he said at last.

"That's right."

The old man continued to pull on his cigarette as if he hadn't heard Héctor's answer, his eyes fixed on some distant point, far beyond the red curtain that hung in the darkness behind the detective's back.

"No. Emiliano Zapata is dead."

"Are you sure, General Zapata?"

*[handwritten margin note: They've now discovered at this point that his father was a revolutionary → from respect]*

"He's dead. I know what I'm talking about. He died in Chinameca in 1919 at the hands of traitors. The same carbines would rise up again today…The same men would give the orders… The people mourned him once already, why should they mourn him again?"

Héctor stood up.

"I'm sorry I bothered you at this time of night."

He held out his hand and the old man took it ceremoniously.

"Don't mention it. Where there's good faith, that's all that matters."

Héctor stepped out past the curtain.

Outside, the black night, a starless sky.

*[handwritten margin note: but is that revolution, in this moment, is dead? or just in hiding?]*

*[handwritten: broken]*

# Afterword

## Incomparable Paco

Great writers by definition are outriders, raiders, sweeping down from wilderness territories to disturb the peace, overturn the status quo and question everything we know to be true—then gone. Like deranged cousins shut away in the houses of loving families, they are a great bother, an embarrassment, open secrets trembling always at the very edge of violence, out there just beyond the light of these campfires we call civilization.

No one quite knows what to do with Paco Taibo. Even in his homeland of Mexico, he says, he's an invisible writer—by which he means unapproved, subversive, and in which he takes obvious pleasure. Meanwhile a disarming arsenal of books continues to tumble from his pen: literary novels, revisionist history, collections of journalism, fictionalized biographies, political essays, detective stories.

It's for the last that he may be best known to readers on this side of the Rio Grande, for whom his work poses, I think, a particular problem.

The book you're holding, *An Easy Thing*, published in 1990 by the prestigious Viking Press whose editors could hardly have failed to be aware of its radical subtext, introduced Paco's work here. Viking followed up a year later with *The Shadow of the*

*Shadow,* an extraordinary novel celebrating the streetcar work-ers' strike in 1922 Mexico City. Neither novel earned much of a foothold on publishing's glass mountain, and Paco soon hopscotched over to The Mysterious Press. Most recently, as one by one his books fell out of print—until this first reissue by The Poisoned Pen Press, at least— he's been published, when published at all, by independent presses such as El Paso's Cinco Puntos, who in 2000 brought out *Just Passing Through.* That novel's fanciful portrait of real-life labor organizer Sebastian San Vicente was an early sketch for *Shadow* and bears every mark of Paco's style: the folding of historical figures into fiction, the persistent, stubborn blurring of boundaries, a tone that trods consistently some unmarked path between the highroad of stridency and the lowlands of melancholy.

It's not only Paco's prolificacy, the variety and very volume of his work, that confuses us. What are we to make of this constant shuttling back and forth from fact to fiction, history to present life, this summa of revolutionary instinct he seems intent upon providing us, Che Guevara rubbing shoulders with Doc Holliday, Mau-Mau with the Musketeers? Is this man a detective-story writer, an avant-garde novelist, the voice of our collective unconscious, a simple contrarian, some half-crazed libertarian Oliver Stone-type, eyes fixed myopically on a handful of moments in history?

U.S. readers in particular, whose knowledge even of their own radical labor movement has been expunged, are unlikely to know much of the general ideas and passions and of the histori-cal movements, specifically Hispanic and Mexican, central to Paco's work. Using the vocabulary available to us, we connect narrative dots, forcing Paco's attitudes and apostrophes to con-form, Procrustes-like, to the closest analog we have, the shape of American leftism, unable to perceive it for the radically different thing it is: anarchism. Anarchism, of course, has a long tradition abroad. But we here in the States have never doubted that every other country at its inmost, secret heart wants nothing more than to be just like us. We would make of them all—think that, given the chance, they would make of themselves—little Americas. Further fundamental differences between "American" quiddities and those from which Paco issues, quickly fall into place.

Unlike the realist American novel, perfectly formed loaves of white bread leavened with irony, the Latin American novel has always been quixotic, playful, self-conscious: a heady mix of coarse grains thrown together on the griddle.

What Paco does, it seems to me, is restore the balance between fabulation and objective social realism. Refusing to dispense with the representational, he refuses also to lash its materials to the mast of likelihood and verisimilitude. Grittily realistic depictions of Mexico City come stepping from the doorways of pure invention. If he wants to have Stan Laurel witness Pancho Villa's assassination or show Leon Trotsky, exiled in Mexico, laboring over authorship of thrillers (Four Hands); if he wants to gather an army of fictive heroes including Sherlock Holmes and the Hound of the Baskervilles, the Earp brothers and Doc Holliday, the Musketeers, the Mau-Mau and the Light Brigade around a victim of the 1968 student-led Mexican uprising (*Calling All Heroes*); if he wants to dovetail Leonardo da Vinci's invention of the bicycle with the theft of a kidney from a Texas female basketball player and usher onstage as investigator a doppelganger of himself or of Héctor Belascoarán Shane (*Leonardo's Bicycle*); if he wants to kill off Shane and in the next book (*No Happy Ending, Return to the Same City*) resurrect him...well, then, he does.

Whatever the story requires.

Paco on Shane's resurrection: "His appearance in these pages is...an act of magic...irrational and disrespectful toward the occupation of writing a mystery series...the story told here belongs to the terrain of absolute fiction, although Mexico is the same and belongs to the terrain of surprising reality."

Story is all, then. And so Paco goes on pulling real rabbits from imaginary hats.

Initially, he says, he turned to crime fiction from a desire to escape the experimentalism then rampant, to find his way back to storytelling. Like many others (Roger Simon or Stephen

Greenleaf in the States, the amazing Jean-Patrick Manchette in France, somewhat later Columbia's Santiago Gamboa), Paco realized that the crime novel gives space and opportunity to address contemporary society as does no other venue, to recreate the actual textures and presence of street life and social levels about him, the flux of assumption and disinformation that keeps the social order afloat, the rifts between reality and appearance that both individual and society must negotiate again and again.

One further spur. Someone told Paco it was impossible to write a crime novel set in Mexico because the crime novel was by its very nature an Anglo genre. Given that, what choice did he have but to write one? Or a dozen?

Again and again here, I've struck out such formalities as *Taibo* and *the author* in favor of, simply, *Paco*. In the cloisters and hallways of my soul I see him striding towards me in Tshirt and leather jacket, Marlboro in one hand, Coke in the other. Uncomfortable at the table of privilege where, attending an international literary conference, he was seated, Paco has escaped. Paco's flown, Paco's once again out and about where he belongs, where all writers belong, at the world's small, crowded, unkempt tables.

Reading, he tells us, the four or five of us there (for we contain multitudes), reading is the most subversive activity in life. Open any true book and you begin to see the world through somebody else's eyes. Nothing is more redeeming than that, or more dangerous.

He believes, too, in the right to myths, the necessity of them. Speaking about Che and other heroes, even small heroes like Héctor Belascoarán Shane, helps us reclaim other rights: our right to romanticism, to adventure, to the sense that our lives are not shallow but infinitely deep, connected to history and to "all those who have no rights, those who suffer abuse their whole lives, people on the margins, the disinherited, the lepers, the poor, the least of the least."

There's the rabbit and the hat, then. And here's Paco Taibo, writer, magician, small hero. The most important postman of all: the one who delivers you to yourself.

James Sallis
Phoenix
January 2002

To receive a free catalog of Poisoned Pen Press titles, please contact us in one of the following ways:

Phone: 1-800-421-3976
Facsimile: 1-480-949-1707
Email: info@poisonedpenpress.com
Website: www.poisonedpenpress.com

Poisoned Pen Press
6962 E. First Ave. Ste 103
Scottsdale, AZ 85251

CPSIA information can be obtained
at www.ICGtesting.com
Printed in the USA
BVHW031419030119
536960BV00001B/59/P

9 781590 580066